M000077361

BOMBING CHICAGO

A NOVEL OF DOMESTIC TERRORISM

BY JERRY JOHNSON

1

Other books by Jerry Johnson:

SEVEN: A Novel of Domestic Terrorism
SIX: A Novel of Domestic Terrorism

All rights reserved.
Copyright © 2019 by Jerry Johnson
This book may not be reproduced in whole
or in part without permission.

"Fighting evil, it's hard work."
-     George W. Bush

Prologue

Thursday, May 14th
Port Hope, Michigan

The 35-foot Bertram crept slowly into the dock slip at the fishing marina in Port Hope. It was still daylight at 9:00 PM on this early spring afternoon in Michigan, but the sun was rapidly headed on its way down over the western horizon. With the rest of the fishing boats already in their docks, the marina was nearly deserted.

Almost every boat was out on the water at daylight, and back in by mid-afternoon, so that fish could be cleaned, and the customers sent on their way with their ice chests full of fish before it got too late to clean the boats. The few remaining captains and mates hanging around the marina that evening were getting seriously into their beer, and

3

paying no attention to this late arriving charter. Pete Hanson's Bertram was a few feet larger than the average boat in Port Hope, and it had attracted some interest when he had first brought it in to port about three years ago. But now it was just another part of the local scenery, and everyone ignored it.

The marina was one of several behind the long breakwater at Port Hope. The official story was that the breakwater was built to give ships a place to make port if the weather got too bad out on Lake Huron, for boats either coming from or headed to the big commercial port in Detroit. The locals all believed that the real story was the breakwater had been built to hide smugglers during prohibition.

Hanson reversed the engines on the *Snow Blower*, and backed the Bertram to a stop just touching the dock at pier five, his rented dock slip. He allowed himself a slight nod at another smuggling run successfully accomplished. Pete had literally grown up in the smuggling business. His great-grandfather had run booze from Canada during prohibition. His grandfather and dad had run drugs and cigarettes, with Pete starting to make runs with his dad at the age of six. What Coast Guard boat would think that a boat captain taking his six-year-old with him on charter fishing trips would be smuggling?

Pete ran some drugs, but rarely, so as not to get noticed, but he was more of an expert in the people smuggling business. He did not bring people into the U.S. too often, and had a select group of customers that appreciated Pete's talent, and liked that he knew how to be discreet. People smuggling was lucrative. The Bertram was paid for, unlike most of the charter boats in the marina, whose captains were still paying on their loans to the Port Hope branch of Bank of America. People smuggling also paid for Pete's vacations to Florida in the winter, and his trips to Vegas during the NCAA March Madness basketball playoffs. His regular fishing charters mostly paid for gas and boat maintenance, a good bit of which he could write off as business expenses on his taxes. No one noticed if he went out with three "fishermen" in the morning, and came back with four that afternoon. People in northeast Michigan had their own problems to worry about, and paid little attention to what others were doing, especially with their boats. Pete was married with two kids, a member of the Chamber of Commerce and the Rotary, and was considered to be a pillar of the community.

The Fair Harbor Marina was unique in that cars and trucks could drive directly down to the slip where their boat was moored, if they knew the gate code to get into the Marina's fenced off parking area. The idea was that each boat captain would enter a specific code for the group chartering that particular boat for the day, but almost everyone in town knew that "9999" was the default code, and individual codes were too much trouble to enter into the system. There were two parking places on the dock for each boat slip. Usually the boat captain got one, with the other reserved for the charter group. If a boat had a mate, he or she had to hoof it up and down from the communal parking lot at the top of the hill overlooking the marina.

In this case Pete had stretched his limit on who he was bringing into the United States, but only because a good customer had leaned on Pete to do so - and paid him ten grand above the going price per person for Pete's extra efforts. Pete had gone out with two customers, and come back with four. The procedure was pretty cut and dried by this point. Two boats would run parallel along the boundary line between the U.S. and Canada, one from each country. The Coast Guard was used to seeing this type of activity on their radar scopes, with fishing boats from the two countries comparing catches and hurling insults about who had the shortest pole. While the Coasties had a blimp up to help with the radar picture, they were more interested in boats crossing the lake from Canada to the U.S. If two boats running parallel along the international border happen to come together for a couple of minutes, most often no one working for the government paid the scene any attention.

This time the transfer between boats was a two-part process. The Canadian boat had a small crane on the back deck, allegedly for hauling in fish nets. In this case, it was used to transfer what looked like a large fish box from the deck of the Canadian boat to the deck of the *Snow Blower*. The seas were running about three feet, but the guys on the Canadian boat knew what they were doing, and the transfer of the box went quickly and smoothly. Pete thought that with the boats rocking back and forth they might have to use the crane to move the two people to his boat, too, but both guys correctly timed the waves and jumped easily into the Port Hope registered boat. One of the guys winced a little when he landed, but he stayed on his feet. The fish box, if opened, showed ice and a couple of just caught King Salmon in the top part of the box, in case some overeager game warden or customs agent type decided to inspect their catch. Just as long as no one ran a Geiger counter over the box while it was open.

The customers called ahead when they got close to shore, and a fifth friend drove down to the marina in his big Dodge Ram Quad Cab pickup. The fact that the pickup had Illinois plates was no big deal at the marina - a lot of the port's charter customers came from that state. With the marina nearly deserted, it was easy for the four customers on the boat to grab the built-in handles on each corner of the fish box, lift it off the boat onto shore, and then from the dock into the bed of the pickup, without the activity being noticed. The shocks on the pickup groaned a little at the additional load, but it was obvious that the truck could handle the extra weight. The pickup had a camper shell over the bed, so the fish box was out of sight as soon as the driver shut the door to the camper. The group's leader handed Pete a satchel, shook his hand, and the five customers piled into the pickup's two seats and drove back up the hill. A little crowded, but the three guys in the back seat of the pickup were not that big, and they were not the type to complain, anyway. They headed south along the coast for a short while, but then turned west to head across the state toward Lake Michigan.

There had been some discussion amongst the group in the pickup about whether to let Pete live after he got the two foreigners smuggled into Michigan. But the final decision had been that eliminating Pete, even if that meant getting rid of a potential witness, would have raised too big a stink. The group wanted to maintain a low profile for as long as possible. Plus, if it was this easy to get people and material into the

Great Satan, there was no reason they could not use the same routine again in the future. The important things were that the team was now complete, the locals had been united with the experts from overseas, and that the first bomb was safely in the United States.

As they headed west, the group leader pulled out a small laptop computer, and prepared a draft email stating simply, "The baby got home safely." An hour later, at three AM local time in Europe, the email account was opened, the draft message read, and then the draft erased. Another innocuous email draft was prepared on a separate account, and this one was read in both the Middle East and Far East later that morning with growing excitement. By using only draft messages the groups hoped to avoid detection by the NSA and others looking for emails going to and from possible terror cells, and the NSA was good at searching for trigger words in every message sent almost anywhere in the world. By only preparing a draft message the actual email was never sent across the Internet - but anyone who had the ID and password of the email account could open the account and read the draft.

The second bomb's surreptitious entry into the United States was a similar operation, but this time no extra people were smuggled into the country. The shrimp boat crept slowly back into its usual dock just south of Houma, Louisiana at about 10:00 Saturday evening. It was foggy, but the tide was up and the boat's captain knew the channel like the back of his hand, so he didn't have to worry about running aground on some outcropping of coral or an oyster mound. The Captain was almost always the one that brought the boat in through the channel, but with the extra cargo this trip he was definitely going to be the man behind the wheel.

The shrimp boat, manned by a Cajun family that had been in the area for over 100 years, had a full load of shrimp the crew had seined out of the Bay of Campeche off the coast of Mexico. And they were also bringing in a "fish box" similar to the one smuggled into Michigan, picked up from a Mexican shrimp boat a couple of nights earlier. This boat, too, occasionally ran some drugs into the U.S. The extended family was large, and there were a lot of mouths that needed feeding, so the captain didn't have any qualms about a little smuggling to help make ends meet. And smuggling was a tradition along this stretch of the Louisiana coast, going back to the days of pirates and other buccaneers.

When the boat was still a couple of miles offshore, the boat's captain picked up his cell from the phone stand next to the ship's wheel, dialed a memorized number, and let it ring three times before hanging up. No message went out over the air, but the ringing phone was notification to the pickup team that the boat was arriving. No calls to the boat from a family member watching the dock and the roads leading to it told the captain that there were no customs or DEA agents in the area, so it would be safe to make the transfer.

This time the reception crew was two big rednecks with short haircuts and multiple tattoos in a dark blue pickup, with a logo on the side of the truck stating that the truck belonged to "Stan's Welding, Dallas, Texas." The pickup team had left their motel room in Houma when they heard the ringing phone, and were waiting on the dock when the boat pulled to a stop next to the quay. The boat captain had a couple of his hands help the customers load the fish box into the pickup, and the pickup was gone before the boat started unloading shrimp. The captain usually helped supervise the start of the unloading process, but he was delayed a little because he went straight to his cabin to store the briefcase of cash handed to him by the guys in the pickup. No email drafts were prepared for this delivery, with the understanding that no news would be good news. Messages were only to be sent if something went wrong.

The bombs had taken nearly four years to design and build, and they were as powerful as the North Koreans could make them without actually using atomic weapons. Four years earlier, while General Shin Tse Kue and Supreme Leader Kim Jong-un were watching the political conventions in the United States to see who would be nominated for President, General Shin commented, "Wouldn't it be nice to wipe out both conventions, and cripple the political superstructure of that entire country?" And an idea was born. The targets would be the next national political conventions, four years away. The sites weren't even picked yet, but the North Koreans started some advance planning for several possible targets.

As it turned out the two sites picked by the political parties were on the Korean's possibility list from the beginning, but the parties did pull a switch. The Republicans opted to go to the McCormick Convention Center in Chicago, even though Chicago was usually considered to be a Democratic stronghold. The idea was to make inroads into Illinois, and to show the country that the Republicans could hold a Chicago convention without riots - something they hoped the television news announcers would be reminding the viewing public about on a regular basis.

The Democrats decided to hold their convention in Dallas. Texas had been a "red" state ever since Lyndon Johnson was buried, but changing demographics had put the state more into play than any time in the last quarter of a century. So, the Democrats decided that going to the Dallas Kay Bailey

Hutchison Convention Center might help flip Texas for this election cycle.

The Koreans could not care less. They planned on bombing both sites. They knew the odds were against getting both bombs in place and exploded at the right time - the Dallas bomb was unlikely to succeed after the first bomb was detonated in Chicago - but the Supreme Leader wanted two bombs, so he got two bombs.

The bombs were designed as dirty bombs. Both were radiological dispersal devices (RDDs), with cesium-137 ground into powder and mixed with the n-octyl phthalate plasticizer that stabilized the plastic explosives in the bombs. If exploded, the bombs would spread the radioactive material as dust over an area approximately a square mile in size, along the lake in Chicago and right in the middle of downtown Dallas, making it nearly impossible to be cleaned, and thus making those two areas uninhabitable for close to a century.

The cesium had been stolen in Hong Kong by a Triad that had worked with the North Koreans many times over the years. The material was smuggled into Nampo via junk transfer (similar to the way the NPRK was getting the bombs into the U.S.), and then transported to an army base outside of Pyongyang where the bombs were to be manufactured. Cesium-137 is used world-wide as a blood irradiator, but then the used material must be disposed of safely. The hospitals in Hong Kong were more than grateful when a new contractor offered to safely remove their used radiological waste at about half the price of their previous waste contractor. The paperwork was perfect, showing that the waste was being properly stored in one of the Far East's best radiological storage locations. No one wanted to check that paperwork too closely, because the deal was saving the various Hong Kong hospitals some big-time *gong baih*.

The North Korean scientists working on the bombs had wanted to use octanitrocubane as the explosive, but found that it was too hard to synthesize in the amounts needed for the bombs and for the testing to be done prior to the bombs being assembled. So, they settled on a mixture of CL-20 and HMX. HMX is one of the most powerful explosives that can be manufactured in bulk, and one that is fairly shock stable. CL-20 (CL is for China Lake, the navy weapons lab in California where the stuff was first synthesized), is fairly unstable by itself, but that explosive is approximately 50% more powerful than HMX. Some people at China Lake worry that a major earthquake in that area could set off the CL-20 they have stored there for research, destroying the entire base.

A smart chemist at the University of Michigan discovered that by using a cocrystalization process he was able to manufacture a better explosive, creating a mix of two CL-20 molecules and one HMX molecule. The new compound was about 20% more powerful than pure HMX, but just about as stable as HMX. Perfect for what the Koreans needed. The chemist, required to publish regularly as part of his faculty duties, was nice enough to send his research, including the cocrystalization procedure, to the highly regarded Chemistry Research Journal – an online magazine that the Korean chemists read every quarter as soon as it was published.

The North Koreans didn't even have to make their own CL-20 and HMX. The French company SNPC makes CL-20, and HMX is available from several different manufacturers. There was the issue of smuggling the explosives into North Korea, but the Koreans have been getting around the sanctions on what can be imported into North Korea for many years. Stuff in diplomatic bags (or boxes marked as diplomatic material) are not subject to inspection or seizure, and over time small amounts of smuggled material can become a large mass of explosives. They tested the stuff in a cave where they had previously done some small atomic bomb testing, and found that the new explosive mixture was more powerful than they had even predicted. The resulting explosion registered on seismic charts across Asia, and the South Koreans started screaming about how the North was again testing atomic weapons.

As the bombs would be radioactive, a lead covering was needed to help avoid triggering some sensitive Geiger counter tracking system while the terrorists were transporting the bombs across the United States from the entry port locations. Most of those radioactivity sensors were set to look for plutonium radioactivity levels, so the thought was that the low radioactive level cesium material, if properly shielded, should be capable of avoiding detection in most instances, except for when the lead shield container was breached.

The bigger issue was that when placed, the bombs could not look like bombs. Both convention locations would be thoroughly searched several times by various security teams, with bomb sniffing dogs checking every room. But the creative Koreans found a possible solution. To take down each convention center, each bomb needed to contain about five hundred pounds of plastic explosives. That, along with the lead shielding and the necessary igniters, timers, and radio receivers, would bring the total weight of each bomb to around seven hundred pounds. Four guys in decent shape can handle that, as long as they use the proper equipment to help move the bombs. So, the fish box delivery systems were created.

But fish boxes would stand out in a convention center, unless the center was hosting a fishing or boating exposition. So, how to disguise the bombs to look like something that belonged in each building?

The answer the Koreans came up with was to disguise the bombs as Rheem water heaters. The Rheem Triton Industrial Water Heater weighs about 775 pounds, so cleaning out the water heating elements and leaving the heater as basically a shell, and adding 500 pounds of explosives and the lead shield, brings the newly disguised bomb back close to its original weight. The Rheem is 26 3/8 inches in diameter, and leaving 1/2 inch for the outside water heater shell meant that the bomb had to be a little over 25 inches across. The Rheem is 77 inches tall, but approximately 10 inches of that total length is a pump and pump motor separate section in the top part of the water heater. So the bombs, including the lead shield, were designed to fit into the 65 inch by 25 inch cylindrical shaped pressure container of the water heater.

If the fake heater was to be opened, it would probably be inspected in that top "pump" section. So, by leaving the pump and motor in place, the water heater would appear to be of normal construction. This particular model includes a full LCD display window that shows that the model is running properly, and how hot the water is in the heater (usually set to 120 degrees in an industrial setting). But a simple software fix by the Koreans meant that the LED display would show the proper numbers if the heater was plugged in to electricity - even if it was not connected to a water source. The best scenario would be for the "plumbers" installing the fake heaters to connect some pipes to the water heaters, so that the heaters would look like they were in service. Plan B was to leave the water heaters in a Rheem box, uninstalled, in some storeroom with other potential spare appliances and parts. All this work took nearly four years to perfect the design, and establish the logistics to get the bombs smuggled into their designated targets. The Koreans knew that there was a good possibility the second bomb would be found after the first explosion. The bomb squads in the U.S. were good at determining exactly where a bomb exploded, and what materials were used to make the bomb. But the Koreans hoped that finding the bomb parts and determining that the bomb was disguised as a water heater would take some time - time enough for the second bomb to be used in Dallas, as the two conventions were set to take place two weeks apart in July and August that summer.

The Koreans loved both the names Rheem and Triton. General Shin, who had spent four years at UCLA and spoke perfect English, had to explain his pun to the Supreme Leader about how the Koreans were going to "Rheem" each political party. Triton, the son of Poseidon in Greek mythology, was known for frightening the Gods when he blew his terrible sounding horn. To the Koreans, who loved their symbolism, those product names were just about perfect.

To smuggle the bombs into the United States the Koreans planned on using a Middle East cutout, to help muddy the waters when the U.S. started investigating who planted the bombs, and a Mexican cartel to help get the second bomb into the United States. North Korean agents had worked for years to establish contacts with U.S. domestic groups that had a big gripe with the government in Washington (the enemy of my enemy is my friend). Working with Islamic Jihadists in the

Midwestern states and with right wing terrorists in Texas to get the bombs in place were fairly simple parts of the overall plan. One need was for welders to take apart the water heaters and reattach the bottoms of the water heaters once the bombs were inside the water heater shell. Another part of the original plan was to recruit contract plumbers that worked at each of the convention centers to deliver and "install" the modified water heaters.

But this plan hit some roadblocks. The McCormick Convention Center in Chicago was a union shop - and they had their own plumbers on staff. The Dallas Convention Center used contract plumbers, but the current contract was with a company that paid their plumbers better than the going rate for the Dallas - Fort Worth Metroplex, so getting hired at that firm was highly competitive. Plus, as it turned out, neither convention center used industrial sized water heaters. Modifications to the original plan were needed.

Research showed that most hotels used industrial sized water heaters. Both convention centers had hotels adjacent to the convention halls, as do most major convention centers around the United States. In Chicago, it was the Hyatt Regency McCormick Place. In Dallas, it was the Omni Dallas Hotel. Both hotels suffered from a high employee turnover rate, and were constantly hiring lower level employees, so it was easy to get a few people hired on staff at both locations. The plan was to wait until each hotel's Chief Engineer was on vacation, and then use the planted employees to help add the water heaters to each hotel's maintenance storage facility deep in the hotel's basement storage area. The plan had some pros and cons. The fake water heaters needed to be put in place some weeks before the conventions were to be held, so as to be less likely to be given a thorough inspection when delivery was made to the hotels, and so they would appear to be just another spare part when the Secret Service started their inspections. But if put in place too early, there was a chance that the Chief Engineer would discover the anomaly, or some maintenance person would actually try to install the fake heater if a real water heater in that hotel quit putting out hot water.

And the North Koreans went to great lengths to ensure that the bombs could not be easily traced back to that small country north of the 38th parallel. They knew that revenge from the United States would be overwhelming if their part in the scheme was laid bare. The bombs were "traded" to Iran for some much-needed oil, and the Iranians were the ones who added the electronics that would start the explosive process. The Iranians added both timers and radio-controlled switches, all manufactured in Germany. They also added detonators made in Eastern Europe. The idea was that when the ATF and FBI bomb guys located enough exploded bomb pieces to try and determine where the bomb originated, the different parts from around the world would make the task of determining the source of the bomb nearly impossible.

The Iranians were the ones with the actual contacts for smuggling material into the United States, having been smuggling opium into the country for years, so the Korean's hands were clean if the bombs were traced back to the smugglers. General Shin thought that he had done everything possible to keep the eventual blame for the bombs from pointing at his country. He knew his life, and his family's survival were at stake if the plan didn't work.

Chapter 1

Friday, May 15th

Both the welder and the plumber had been recruited locally for the job. They all attended the same mosque, and it was easy to feel people out during discussions on faith, to determine who would make a good convert for the cause. They started on the bomb renovation early Friday morning. They had planned on it taking two days, but hoped they could finish in one. No one wanted to spend any more time around the radioactive material than they had to. They were all, at least philosophically, willing to give their life for the cause. But they also all thought that maybe Allah had more for them to do than to die in the next two weeks from a radiation overdose.

They set up in the safe house's garage, with both guys wearing gloves and lead lined aprons, and breathing from a portable oxygen tank. They had to be careful with the welding torch and the oxygen, but the welder was experienced and knew how to handle the issue.

Abriz, the team leader, and Hamid had helped the two craftsmen to get the water heater up on sawhorses. The welder easily sliced around the bottom rim of the heater, removing the base plate, while the plumber started removing the hose connections leading to the heater's interior from the sides and the top of the heater. Once the base plate and hose connections had been removed, it was easy to pull the long heater element out of the base of the water heater, since that was the way it had been originally installed. Now they had an empty shell, and they were ready for the hard part.

Abriz and Hamid came back into the garage, and with everyone shielded and masked, they opened the fish box and lifted the bomb, in its lead shielding, out of the foam cushion where it had been riding. They slowly and carefully slid it into the water heater shell until it reached the top section of the heater, where the pump was mounted.

The welder very carefully and slowly rewelded the base plate back onto the water heater cylinder. He didn't want to overheat the interior of the cylinder, so he had to take his time, even if it meant a little more exposure to the radioactive isotopes in the bomb. The bomb did have its own lead shield, but the welder and plumber were still worried about possible contamination. The outside hose connections were reattached by the plumber. The transformation was almost complete.

Abriz was the bomb expert. He had the plumber remove the plate between the pump and the new bomb - it was just screwed into place - and Abriz attached the battery that, when the correct wires were attached, would make the water heater's LED display come to life. He had a second battery to add, to power the radio control bomb activator and the bomb's detonator pack. But that electronic source would be kept separate until it was time to put the bomb in place, just as another security precaution. Abriz didn't want to go by some construction site on the drive back across Michigan and have some radio signal prematurely detonate his bomb. By 6:00 PM Friday night the bomb was ready, well ahead of schedule.

The bomb was placed in a specially designed carrying rack in the back of Abriz' pickup by the four terrorists. It again weighed over 700 pounds, so it took everyone's help to get it into the storage rack. The team used ropes placed under the cylinder to lift it from the sawhorses, and to get it into the back of the pickup. They also loaded the welding equipment and the heater element they had pulled from the water heater. It was a little difficult to get the modified heater in through the rear door of the camper shell, but the shell was necessary to help hide the heater from prying eyes. The "water heater" was hidden from view when the back door of the camper shell was shut. Everyone went back into the house to take a long shower, to wash off any possible radioactive residue.

Abriz had set up an over watch on the house, putting an observer at the top of the hill overlooking the rental facility. He didn't think there was much of a chance of them being discovered, but he wanted some warning if the cops showed any interest in the place. Abdul, the fifth team member, had volunteered for the first shift - which also meant he didn't have to handle the bomb. Now that the bomb was loaded, Abriz went to four-hour shifts for his team, to make sure there was always someone with a walkie-talkie radio watching the neighborhood.

The same procedure was followed at a ranch outside of Forney, Texas, about twenty miles east of Dallas. The crew there modified the water heater, loaded everything into a different pickup, and moved to a safe house in Mesquite, even closer to Dallas. The Stan's Welding pickup was left in the garage at the ranch house in Forney, hidden from view. This team was able to take their time, and did a better job of cleaning up everything before moving on to Mesquite.

Both bombs were now ready to be armed and placed at their targets.

Chapter 2

Chief of Police John Bradley was having a great day. Right up until the guy with the shotgun tried to blow him away. The Chief had spent some time that Saturday morning thinking about how great things were going in his life. He had a job he loved, having been appointed head cop for the town of Grant the previous year. He had a staff of six officers, two on each shift, and that along with his admin assistant and dispatchers was as big a staff as he wanted. John was a firm believer in the Peter Principle, and he could not see himself as the Chief of Police in New York or Miami - or even in Grand Rapids, the nearest "big" Michigan city. He didn't want the politics or headaches that would be part of managing a bigger city's police force, and he realized that just because he was good at his current job did not mean that he would excel in a bigger location.

John had taken a patrol shift that Saturday morning, to allow one of his younger officers to attend the officer's oldest son's first little league baseball game. John didn't have to do much during a normally quiet Saturday shift - just drive around town and check things at the schools, and he spent a couple of hours just parked on Highway M-37 at the southern end of town, watching for speeders headed north to the lakes. He really didn't want to issue any tickets, but just by being there the patrol car was a deterrent for people coming into town, where the speed limit dropped from 55 to 40, and then all the way to 30 miles per hour when you got closer to the two-block downtown area. He wasn't going to pull anyone over unless they were doing about 60, or obviously high or intoxicated.

He spent his time while parked in the car thinking back to how he had gotten where he was, and how lucky his life had been. John had gone into the army after graduating from Michigan State, and had served three tours in Afghanistan. He had found while in college that he had an affinity for languages, and when he got to his assignment he found that he picked up both Dari and Pashto fairly easily. That language ability got him promoted to Captain above the zone when he went back for his second tour, and he often served as his unit's interpreter. Not having to lean on a "local" interpreter meant not only more accurate information for his squad, but information that could be much more trustworthy. By his third tour he was a major, assigned as a Military Police liaison to the local CIA contingency group. John found that he liked the idea of solving crimes, but didn't like the methods used by the CIA to get information from suspects. So, after that tour ended, he resigned his commission and went back to Michigan. He found an opening as a deputy sheriff in the Newaygo County Sheriff's Office, close to where his wife's parents lived on Lake Emerald, and it was only a couple of years before he applied for and got the Chief's job just eight miles down the road in Grant.

John's wife Cathy called just before his shift ended. "Remember that we volunteered to run the concession stand at Carolyn's softball game tonight?"

"No, I haven't forgotten (he had, but he wasn't going to admit that to his wife). What do you need?"

"I need you to go to Gene's and pick up hotdogs, buns, and brats. We will need to grill everything this afternoon, and be ready to get to the high school by 6:30 or so. We have parents making cookies and brownies, and they are going to meet us at the concession stand before the game starts. I'll get the popcorn machine at the stand going as soon as we get there. We have Glen and Pete from the football team helping us in the booth tonight, so expect a lot of teenage girls wanting to buy hot dogs!"

John grumbled, but he knew that all the softball team parents had to take a turn in the concession stand, and he was glad they had waited to get their turn in the barrel out of the way at the end of the season, when the weather was definitely better. He promised to get everything they needed. "Okay, no problem. I'll call you if I have any questions about what to get. Love you."

"Love you, too. Call me when you're headed home and I'll get the grill going." She wasn't sure he heard the last part because he had already clicked the off button on his cell phone.

John returned the patrol car to police headquarters at the town's administration office, checked in with his replacement on the afternoon shift, and got into his own car and headed up the street to Gene's Family Market - the only grocery store in Grant.

He had his grocery cart about half full of the supplies they needed for the concession stand work, and was looking at condiments, when a four-year-old boy whizzed by him, pushing a child-sized grocery cart at full speed down the aisle. John looked up, and saw the boy's mother at the end of his aisle, looking defeated at the thought of trying to keep up with her son. John knew the lady slightly - the two families attended the same church in Grant - so he smiled at her and nodded, knowingly. She just shrugged and shook her head. John wanted to laugh, but knew that wasn't the right reaction, so he just kept quiet.

The boy sped around the corner at the end of the grocery aisle and John heard a crash from the next aisle over, and someone started cussing. John knew the kid had run into someone, but what was interesting was that the conversation he overheard was in Pashto.

"Dammit! That stupid kid just ran into my bad knee - the one I hurt in that training exercise last week in Syria."

Another voice answered, also in Pashto. "I told you, English only!"

"I know, but it just came out when that idiot ran into me. Whatever happened to controlling your kids when you shop? When I was his age, I never ran around and hurt someone when at the souk."

John was tempted to turn the corner at the end of the aisle and get a look at the two people involved in the conversation, but his cop instincts kicked in. He was still in uniform, and he didn't want to panic the guys he had overheard. He didn't know what they might do if a cop suddenly appeared at the end of their aisle. He headed the other way, to the checkout stand, and quickly got his groceries scanned and sacked. He did catch a glimpse of the two people in the mirrors over the checkout stands. As he suspected, two people of Middle Eastern descent, with one looking to be about 5-10, and the other about 5-7. Both were wearing polo shirts and shorts, looking like typical summer tourists out on a grocery run. If John had not heard the conversation, he would not have given them a second glance.

John got back out to his car, and threw the groceries in the back seat. He yanked out his cell phone, and called his dispatcher back at police headquarters.

"Hey, John. Why are you calling me on your cell instead of using your police band?

"Jim, listen to me closely. First of all, turn on the call recorder immediately, and start recording this call."

"Done."

"OK. Don't say anything, just listen. Here's what I have. Two people in Gene's, Middle Eastern descent, speaking Pashto. And one of them talked about being in a training camp in Syria last week. As weird as it sounds, we might have a terrorist cell right here in Grant. I can't think of any other reason why we would have people that were in Syria last week here in Michigan. I'm not using the police radio because their friends might be monitoring the police bands in the area. I'm back in my car, and I'm going to put the phone down on the seat, in speaker mode, so that you can hear me talk. I'm going to try to follow them back to wherever they are staying, but I don't want to do so holding a cell phone while driving. Don't try and bring in any backup just yet. Let me reconnoiter the situation and then we'll determine how we want to proceed."

Jim was silent for a moment. "Holy shit," was his quiet response. "Be careful."

John pulled out of the parking lot of Gene's, and into the gas station lot beside the grocery store. He didn't want to make it too obvious that he was following the guys he had overheard in the store, but he didn't want to lose them, either. If they turned back south from Gene's, darting between the fairly steady stream of cars headed north, John would have a harder time following - but he didn't want to be right behind them, either. But when the two guys came out of Gene's they did turn north, going through the light in Grant and heading on up M-37 toward Newaygo. John let a few cars go by, and then pulled into the traffic to follow.

John spoke a little loudly to make sure he was heard on the speaker phone over the car noise. He had the car windows rolled up to try and hold down the road noise. It was getting warm in the car, but he didn't notice. "Blue Dodge Ram Quad Cab, Illinois plates, white camper shell on the back of the truck. I didn't get close enough to get the plate number. Just the two guys, headed north on 37. There was some sort of logo on the driver's door of the pickup - I'll try and get that if I can get closer." He gave Jim the description of the suspects from what John had seen in the mirror at Gene's.

Jim responded, "10-4," just so that John would know that Jim was still on the other end of the call.

John tried to verbalize his thoughts as he drove, trying to remember exactly what was said in Gene's. He relayed the overheard conversation almost verbatim, just to make sure it was on record while he still had it fresh in his mind. He knew that getting that on the recording would be necessary as evidence if and when he went for a search warrant for the suspected terrorists' safe house. "Pickup is turning east on 88th, heading toward the Hess Lake area. Maybe they are renting one of the places on Hess or Brooks Lake?" John turned right on 88th after them, but still tried to keep back about two hundred yards. 88th was pretty busy during the spring, as people came to the lakes to open their lake houses, and get their docks and boats in the water, so there was other traffic. John didn't think he had been made by his suspects, as he was already starting to call them in his mind. Hess Lake was actually in the Newaygo Police Department's area of responsibility, but John was not about to let the sometimes-rival department get the credit for shutting down a potential terrorist cell.

The pickup turned right off 88th onto Parkwood Drive, just before reaching the Hess Lake Party Store. John stopped at the intersection of 88th and Parkwood, because he knew that Parkwood was only a block long, and he thought that following the truck onto Parkwood would be a little too obvious. John turned around in the Party Store's parking lot, and pulled off 88th on the north side of the road, with the car snuggled in next to the corn field on that side of the street.

He released his seatbelt, twisted, and grabbed his binoculars from the back seat of his car, keeping his eyes on the pickup. He watched the vehicle pull into a house right on the lake, at the intersection of Parkwood and Lockwood Ct.

John was located on higher ground, as the street sloped down from the corn field toward the lake, so he had a good view of the house. He could see a second vehicle, a small Ford SUV, in the house's gravel driveway, but the garage door was closed, and he couldn't determine if there were more than the two vehicles at the house. John still had the phone on the seat beside him, as he was using both hands to steady the binoculars. He was telling Jim that the two guys had parked the pickup and were headed into the house when the guy with the shotgun blasted away at John, shooting through the car's passenger window.

John had made one mistake - forgetting to check his "six." He had been trained in the military to always watch for people trying to sneak up from behind, but in his excitement he had forgotten this standard strategy, and it cost him. The high ground had been staked out by the terrorists, too. They had deployed a lookout at the top of the hill, hiding in the corn field.

Hamid came sprinting back down the hill to the safe house, still carrying his shotgun. He ran in through the door that was already being opened by one of the guys inside the house, and yelled, "I shot the sheriff!"

Abriz, the group's nominal leader, grabbed Hamid and took the gun away from him. Hamid looked hurt, but Abriz told him, "Just to keep someone else from getting shot by mistake. Now, what have you done?"

Hamid, half out of breath, stammered, "I recognized the Grant policeman from the pictures we saw during the briefing we had been given about law enforcement in the area when we were in Syria. He had obviously followed you back to the house, and was watching through binoculars. We may be about to be raided, so I killed him to try and give us a little time."

Abriz took a deep breath. By this time, all four team members were gathered around their leader. "OK, the bomb has already been loaded back into the pickup. We're lucky that the welder has finished resealing the water heater shell. Pack up everything you can into the two vehicles, and we need to be out of here in three minutes. You know the planned escape routes. Hamid, you drive the SUV and go north to the stoplight at 82, and then east over to 131. I'll drive the pickup, and cut west on 82 through Fremont and then head over toward Muskegon. We'll meet back tonight at the safe house in Chicago. Make sure you are not being followed!" Four minutes later both vehicles pulled out of the driveway, and the house was left abandoned.

If Hamid had been using a deer slug in his shotgun, he would have blown John's head completely apart. But Hamid had bird shot loaded in the gun, and the passenger window on John's car had deflected a lot of pellets. Enough got through the window to cut John up pretty badly, and the force of the blast knocked his head against the driver's door, giving him a concussion. He fell back onto the front seat of the car. Hamid had taken a quick look, seen John prone on the seat and bleeding profusely, and assumed that John was dead or dying. Head wounds tend to bleed a lot, and the car seat was already soaked in blood. Hamid had tried the passenger car door, but it was locked, and he didn't want to try and reach through the glass remaining in the busted window to get to the door lock.

John had fallen on top of the cell phone, and Hamid did not see it. The call was still open. Jim heard the shotgun blast, and tried a couple of times to get John to respond. Then Jim started throwing switches on his radio console. "All units - shots fired, officer possibly down. Corner of 88th and Parkwood, out by Hess Lake. Newaygo Police and County Sheriff's office, if you have people close by, please respond. State Police, if you have anyone on 37, let me know. Be advised that suspects were driving a blue Dodge Ram Quad Cab, Illinois plates, number unknown. Suspects were of Middle Eastern descent, one approximately 5-10, the other approximately 5-7. Both were dressed in polos and shorts. Shots were fired less than two minutes ago, so suspects have to still be in the area. Please consider them armed and dangerous." Jim knew that his call would also get an ambulance headed toward the scene. He started getting responses immediately.

The first car to reach the scene was a Newaygo Police cruiser. That officer had just reached John's car when a State Police cruiser also pulled up. Both officers were just getting John out of his car when the ambulance arrived, so they let the EMTs take over trying to save John. The two cops turned toward the house down the hill. No one could be seen at the house, but the two cops didn't know what they were facing. They barricaded the road with their vehicles, and waited for reinforcements. Traffic was starting to build up on 88th behind what was now a crime scene, so the next car to arrive, a Grant police car, was sent to divert traffic. Another Newaygo Sheriff's Office cruiser arrived, and that officer was sent to the east end of Lockwood, to make sure that no one escaped in that direction.

The house looked empty. Within twenty minutes a State Police Officer had tracked down the house owners, and they said they rented through a local rental management company. The company was contacted, and luckily they were in the office that Saturday, as that is when a lot of renters begin and end their rental week. The current renter's information for the suspect's address was pulled, but the Illinois driver's license that had been used as ID for the rental turned out to be a fake. The credit card used for the rental was being traced, but that would take some time.

Now that several cops were on the scene, they debated whether or not they needed to call in a SWAT team. Newaygo County had a team and a tank like SWAT vehicle, but getting things in place would take an additional thirty minutes, and the officers decided not to wait. The cops did approach the house cautiously, just in case, and took some quick glances through the windows. No one could be seen, so they put people by the back door and busted in from both directions simultaneously. The place was empty, but the officers could see signs of a quick abandonment. After the cops cleared the house, they pulled back out and waited for a state crime scene team to come in for a more thorough investigation.

The good news, if there was any, was that John Bradley had made it to the hospital in

Fremont alive. He had lost a lot of blood, and had been taken immediately into surgery. The doctors were not commenting or giving a prognosis, but at least getting John to the hospital while still breathing was a start. The Grant Deputy Chief, Tom Summers, went himself to notify Cathy about the shooting, and to take her and the kids to Fremont so that they could be there when there was news from the doctors about John's condition.

The bad news was that there was no sign of the suspects. No one could locate the pickup or the sedan that John had described when he first reached the house off 88th, even with roadblocks being quickly established on almost every road leading out of the area. The shooter or shooters had vanished into the west Michigan haze. The cops didn't know if the suspects had fled to another nearby safe house, or if they had beaten the roadblocks out of the area.

Chapter 3

Sunday, May 17th

Bill Peterson thought he might be in over his head. As the new Special Agent in Charge of the Chicago office of the FBI, Bill kept telling himself that he wasn't in Phoenix any longer. Except for some reason it kept coming out "Kansas" in his mind. Bill was in the office on a Sunday just trying to catch up with the written briefings his staff had given him on their current caseloads - everything from human trafficking to bank robberies. He had undercover agents that he had not yet met, and wasn't even sure how he was going to arrange meetings with some of those agents, as deeply as they were imbedded with some gangs or potential terrorist groups.

There were a few other agents in the office when Bill had come in that Saturday morning, and when his phone rang on his desk, he thought it was just another agent trying to get some time alone with him to pitch a project. But when he answered, Bill's priorities shifted again.

"This is Bill." When he heard the voice on the other end of the line he almost came to attention. "I'm fine, just getting settled in. And how are you, Mr. Director?" Bill had never gotten a call directly from the FBI Director, and wasn't sure about the protocol - he had not been briefed on this possibility!

The Director got straight to the point. "Have you heard anything about the police chief that got shot yesterday up in Michigan, who thought he might have stumbled onto some sort of terrorist plot out in the middle of nowhere?"

"Yes, sir." Bill almost chuckled. He had seen the report from the Michigan State Police, but had not thought much about it. If anything, he had thought it was probably just another drug bust that went south. Bill had his own problem cases to worry about.

The Director cut him off. "Well, late last night some bright CSI type got out his Geiger counter, just to check off another box on the investigation worksheet, but then the machine went crazy out in the garage where these alleged assholes were staying. They have something very radioactive, and this is now your number one case. Get a team together, get up there to Bumfuck, Michigan, and then email me with your thoughts. We need to stop this cell before they can pounce. I want to hear back from you daily on this, starting tomorrow. The truck they were using had Illinois plates. They may be headed your way. You have shown good gut instincts in your earlier assignments. That is one reason I put you in Chicago. Use those instincts, and find these critters."

The phone went dead before Bill could get out another, "Yes, sir."

By Sunday afternoon Bill was approaching Grant, Michigan, with four of his agents. He could have just sent the team, but the phone call from the Director had seemed to indicate that the boss wanted Bill directly hands on for this case. Besides, they had taken one of the Bureau's Ford Expeditions for the road trip (Bill remembered that Dave Barry called the big SUV the "Subdivision") so there was plenty of room in the vehicle.

Bill had wanted to bring his second in command on the road trip, but Chet Kingsley, the ASAC and former acting Director until Bill had gotten to Chicago, begged off when Bill called to see if Chet wanted to go. Chet had been in an accident several months back, breaking his left arm and a couple of ribs, and hurting his back. He had been out of the office on sick leave quite a bit since the accident, and had seemed to be on the road to recovery. He had been back in the office on "light duty" for about six weeks, but he had recently suffered a relapse - Chet's back had gone out on him again, just before Bill got to town.

Bill had a lot of sympathy for Chet. Bill had hurt his back playing baseball back in his college days at the University of Texas, when he fielded a bunt from the pitcher's mound and twisted to make the throw to first base. That had taken place in October, during fall practice, and it had been the next March before Bill was able to throw without pain. When Bill heard about Chet, he called him and told him to take all the time he needed to recover. "It took me six months to get my back better, and I was 19 at the time. I can't imagine trying to get over something like that at thirty-five. So do your rehab and get better. We'll hold down the fort at the office until you feel ready to come back."

Bill continued to go over briefing papers while another agent drove, so Bill was at least getting some work done during the trip north on Interstate 196. He also reviewed what little they knew about the Michigan case. It looked like the Police Chief that had gotten himself shot would recover - he was still listed in "guarded" condition at the hospital, mostly because of his concussion - and the concussion had apparently robbed the Chief of his short term memory of the Saturday events. About all the FBI had was a copy of the recorded conversation between the Chief and his dispatcher, and the notes from the Michigan CSI team that had investigated the crime scene. Bill hoped they could eventually interview the Chief, once he had recovered enough to sit for questioning, but the trip was mainly to get a feel for the safe house, and to try and determine why the suspects had ended up in western Michigan.

Bill's big questions were about the "fish box" found in the house's garage, and why the box was radioactive. The CSI team had talked about how the box had a false bottom, with the area under the shelf used to hold fish being cushioned with foam rubber. There was a distinct shape of a cylinder impressed into that foam. Bill wanted the FBI lab to check out every part of the box - where the parts of the box came from, if the construction of the box itself was common to some particular area of the world, and he had a lot of other unanswered questions. Why was the box left in the garage? Was that an oversight during their rush to escape the safe house, or were the suspects done with whatever reason they were using the box? A "fish box" probably meant something was carried in on a boat. Where did that boat land? Which boat? What else did the boat smuggle into the United States, if something (or someone) was smuggled? Could the weight of whatever was in the box be determined by the depth of the impressions in the foam rubber? Any residue left in the foam from whatever was in the box? Would the local gendarmerie be willing to let the FBI lab take the lead on investigating the box? Some police forces got along well with the FBI, but Bill knew that, unfortunately, the FBI had a tendency to run roughshod over the locals when the Bureau was taking over a case, and Bill didn't know how the local and Michigan state cops had been treated in their previous dealings with the Bureau.

Bill had applied his gut instincts, as requested by the Director, and ordered a computer review of all the camera recordings of vehicles headed south from Michigan into Illinois since the shooting. Bill even had the cameras on the ferries taking cars across Lake Michigan to Wisconsin checked, in case the suspects decided to try that route back to whatever place they were headed. Most major highways have regular camera setups at various intervals, and the state line was one favorite camera location. The review had turned up eighteen Dodge pickups with Illinois plates headed south from Michigan, on various highways, during the last 24 hours, and agents had been dispatched to find the vehicle owners and find out why they had been in Michigan. Bill hoped to have those results by midnight Sunday night - one thing the FBI was good at was throwing a lot of manpower at an important case.

Bill had also taken a quick look at Michigan geography and the surrounding areas. He knew that Lake Michigan was completely within the U.S. borders, and a boat coming into Lake Michigan from Lake Huron or points further east would have had to pass through the locks between the two lakes. He thought that was doubtful, and it was also unlikely that the smuggler's ship had come all the way down the Saint Lawrence Seaway from the Atlantic to Detroit. Another possibility was that the box came across Lake Michigan from Wisconsin, but that seemed to be an unlikely detour, if the suspects were from Illinois. It was much more likely the fish box had been smuggled in from Canada. That meant it had to come into Michigan, if it came directly into Michigan, which he thought likely, into an eastern Michigan port on Lake Huron. As soon as his staff had identified which pickup was the one probably being driven by the suspects, he was going to get the computer nerds to find that license plate on camera going to or coming from some Michigan port city.

The FBI team found the Grant area, and the house itself, to be pretty nondescript.

The area was full of lake enthusiasts during the summer months, and to Bill that meant a great hiding place for the suspects. Lots of strangers in the area meant that no one would pay any attention to a few more. The lead CSI investigator was still on the scene when the FBI team arrived, and gave the team a quick tour. "The suspects were pretty professional in their clean up before they fled. They even took their garbage with them. We even found that they had poured cleaning solution down the various house drains, to keep us from finding any usable DNA. Every surface had been wiped, and the floors vacuumed. They took the vacuum bag with them. I doubt the cleaning crew that cleans the house between renters does as good a job as these guys."

Sam Collins, the Michigan State Police's CSI team leader, continued as they walked through the house and yard. "We have left the garage pretty much just as we found it, since that seems to be the crux of our evidence. Besides the fish box, we have found ground up slag residue on the floor of the garage, leading us to believe that someone had been welding in that building.

Other than that, it looks like a typical garage, with yard tools, hoses, snow shovels, and other junk you typically find in any garage." Bill asked about getting access to the stuff found so that the FBI lab could take a look at everything, and Sam replied, "I already asked about that. The governor himself got a call from the FBI Director, and we are to give you anything you want. We've already sent samples to our lab in Lansing, but I know you have better equipment than we do, so I'm happy to get your guys to look at this stuff, too. Of course, we would like to see whatever you find - this is still, officially, our case." Bill readily agreed to make sure the locals got a copy of anything the FBI lab developed.

He looked around the garage, wondering what had been finished there, and why it had to be done after the radioactive material arrived in Michigan. He didn't see anything unusual about the garage or the house. The empty fish box, now shoved up against a garage wall, was a lot larger than the normal sized fish storage ice chest found on most charter boats. The water hoses and other tools in the garage were standard for the area. There was a pile of unfolded cardboard boxes up against one wall, stacked on edge behind an empty recycling bin. The interior garage ceiling was unfinished, and there were a few pieces of lumber stored in the rafters, along with some very old looking fishing poles. There were no windows in the garage overhead door, so no one would have been able to see what was going on in the garage with that door shut. The slag dust on the concrete floor of the garage was not visible to the naked eye, and the CSI team had done a good job of identifying that material so quickly.

If the CSI guy had not found radioactivity, this would have just been another drug bust gone bad in the eyes of cops everywhere, and the FBI would never have gotten involved. But the Geiger counter clicks had turned this into a critical national security case, and Bill knew he probably only had limited time to solve this before some vital piece of real estate became unusable for a few hundred years. The only good news was that the finding of radioactivity had not leaked to the press, so there was not a horde of reporters screaming questions from the end of the block. He turned to his team and said, "Seen enough? Let's go." And they headed back south.

Chapter 4

Monday, May 18th

Tommy Gaspard had always wanted to be a Marine. Tommy's dad had been a big John Wayne fan, and had several of his movies on VCR tapes when Tommy was growing up. From "The Sands of Iwo Jima" to "Flying Leathernecks," Tommy was hooked. He read everything he could about the Marine Corps, and even learned the words to the Marine Hymn.

His dream was reinforced when, in the 8th grade, his entire class took a field trip to Washington, D.C. Two memorable things happened to Tommy on that trip. The most memorable actually occurred when it was getting dark on the way home, when after a stop at a McDonald's in West Virginia for dinner, Tammy Devereux came to the back of the charter bus where Tommy was sitting, said, "Is this seat taken?" and sat down beside him. Tommy was on his Middle School's football team, and knew the girl as one of the cheerleaders that yelled for the team from the sidelines on Thursday nights when the Middle School games were played.

When the bus headed out, and the driver turned the interior bus lights down low so that people could sleep, Tammy got up, reached into her backpack stored on the rack above them, and pulled out a blanket. She pulled it over both of them, and then raised the middle arm rest between the two bus seats. She leaned her head over on Tommy's shoulder, and pretended to be going to sleep. Tommy looked around, saw that no one was paying them any attention, and that the trip chaperones were all at the front of the bus, either sleeping or reading. He slipped his arm around Tammy, and before he knew it Tammy had her tongue down his throat. She allowed him to put his hand under her sweater, since they were hidden under the blanket, but wouldn't let him go any further. She whispered, "We might get caught!" But Tommy knew he would never forget that night.

The second memorable thing from the trip, at least to Tommy, was seeing the Friday night Retreat Parade at the Marine Barracks at 8th & I in Washington. The Marines performed close order drill, the Marine Band played, the troops lowered the American and Marine flags, and the band closed the ceremony with the playing of Taps. Tommy ended up with tears in his eyes, and he wasn't the only one there with a handkerchief. When his class had to write the standard "What I saw in D.C." essay after returning to school, this is what he led off with in his report. Others might have been more impressed with the Lincoln or Washington monuments, or even sitting in the gallery at the House of Representatives (which Tommy thought was immensely boring), but the Marines, along with Tammy, made the trip worthwhile as far as Tommy was concerned.

Tommy originally planned on being a Marine fighter pilot - but after discovering that he would have to graduate college to become an officer, and when he learned the odds of actually getting into a jet, he changed his goal to getting into Force Recon. Force Recon Marines are part of the Marine's Special Operations Command, and they are the Marine version of the Navy SEAL teams. Force Recon troops specialize in amphibious operations such as seizing captured ships from pirates off the coast of Africa, and deep reconnaissance behind enemy lines. The training is rigorous, and you have to be a damn good Marine just to be considered for Recon. But Tommy was in great shape after working weekends and every summer on his uncle's shrimp boat, and he knew he could meet the physical challenges of the position. And he was determined to make it through the mental ones, too.

Today was a big day for Tommy. He had just graduated from High School, and he had taken his old pickup to the Marine Recruiting Office and the Military Entrance Processing Station in New Orleans, to take the Armed Services Vocational Aptitude Battery test. He knew he had to score at least a 105 on the GT (General Technical, including Arithmetic Reasoning) portion of the ASVAB to be eligible for Force Recon, but Tommy wasn't worried about the test - he had always done well in math. Tommy thought about his trip to D.C. and seeing the Marine's Retreat Formation as he drove north towards New Orleans. He wondered if he would ever be assigned as part of that formation. He knew he didn't play a musical instrument, and so he wasn't going to be in the Marine Band - so getting there as a good Marine was the only way he would ever see Eighth & I. He also thought briefly about Tammy Devereux. She hadn't crossed his mind in years. She had dropped out of Houma High School during their junior year, pregnant by the 25-year-old trucker she had been dating. The last Tommy had heard, they had gotten married and moved to Baton Rouge. Tommy knew that Tammy had been using him that night on the bus, whether out of boredom or for some other reason he didn't understand, but he didn't have any complaints. He continued to play various sports through his high school years, and enjoyed the company of several girlfriends during those years, even taking the homecoming queen to their senior prom. But no one wanted to get serious with him, because the girls all knew he was leaving town as soon as he graduated and turned eighteen. As he drove, he thought to himself how glad all of that was now behind him, and he was finally ready to start his career.

The Marine Recruiter had told Tommy on a previous visit to the recruiting depot that the

Marines preferred seasoned veterans for Recon - at last three years of service and a couple of promotions before they would normally even let candidates for Recon submit an application - but that a shortage of people applying had forced the Marine brass to start letting people apply as soon as they had finished Boot Camp and School of Infantry (SOI) training.   The recruiter told Tommy that going straight to Recon would be challenging. "You don't have to be the outstanding Boot or number one in your SOI class, but you need to be damn close if you want that 0321 MOS (Military Occupational Specialty) and a ticket straight to Camp Pendleton's Basic Recon Course when you get out of SOI."

Tommy did well on the test, as he knew he would, but he did have a problem. And he had always heard that if you have a problem in the Marines, you take it to your Sargent. So that is exactly what he did. He finished the test, and then waited until the other two potential recruits had finished their exams and turned them in to the guy with a lot of stripes on his sleeves that had been proctoring the test. "Sir, can I ask you about something?"

The Sargent glared at Tommy, but then remembered that this was still a potential recruit, so his features softened. "Kid, I'm going to tell you this now, to save you a reaming from your boot camp gunny. I am not an officer, and only officers are called 'Sir.' I got my rank by working my ass off and getting some experience in some very hairy places - not by sitting on my behind at some country club college. If you turn out to be a good Marine, and I think you will, after you get a couple of promotions you can call me gunny. Right now, you call me Sargent, or Gunnery Sargent - but you NEVER call me 'Sir.' You got that?"

Tommy turned a little pale, and stammered, "Yes, Si-Sargent." The Sargent grinned at him. "Better. Okay, what can I help you with?"

Tommy swallowed, but then looked the Sargent right in the eye. "You know I work some weekends and most of the summer for my uncle, the shrimper. Well, sometimes he brings in more than shrimp."

The Sargent interrupted Tommy. "You mean he smuggles drugs?"

"Yes, Sargent. But never when I was aboard. So, I wasn't involved. Until this last weekend. We picked up this huge fish box from a Mexican shrimper, and brought it back with us. The thing had to weigh about half a ton. We used our crane to help pull it off our boat, and it took four of us to help manhandle the box into the back of the pickup that was there to pick up the box when we docked. The box was nearly ten feet long, and the shocks on the pickup really groaned when we dropped the box in the bed.

Now, I want you to know that when we picked it up we were told to never open the lid on the box, so I don't know for sure that it contained drugs - but I suspected. The pickup was a Ford F-150, blue, with 'Stan's Welding, Dallas, Texas' on the doors. Two big guys were in the pickup, and they helped us load the fish box.

My problem is that when I was filling out the e-QIP form for my security clearance, back about 100 pages into the questionnaire it asks," and here Tommy read off a sheet of paper he had brought with him, "Have you been involved with the transfer, shipping, handling, or sale of any drug or controlled substance? I don't know whether to answer yes or no. I SUSPECT the fish box was full of drugs, but I always thought that drugs were pretty light weight. And I never saw any drugs. So how do I fill out the form? I want to be honest, because I know that lying on the form can get you disqualified. But if I answer yes, I've been involved in smuggling drugs, that will get me disqualified, too. So, what is your advice on how I should answer that question?"

The Sargent thought for a minute. "Tell them no, you have never smuggled drugs. It wasn't your boat, you didn't profit from the operation, other than to get paid as a deckhand, and, like you say, you don't know for sure that there were drugs in the fish box. You don't need to be disqualified for some stupid stunt your uncle is pulling."

Tommy sighed with relief. "Thanks, Gunny!" The Sargent didn't bother to correct him.

After Tommy had headed back south towards Houma, the Sargent started thinking about the wild tale he had heard from the recruit. Sargent Ken Miles had a brother that was an agent in the New Orleans DEA office. Ken called his brother. "Ben, you got a minute?" Ken relayed the story, and his brother promised to follow up.

Chapter 5

Tuesday, May 19th

Bill Peterson was thinking about how to handle a major personnel problem as he walked to the cafeteria for a cup of coffee. He could have had his administrative assistant, Cindy, bring him coffee, but he knew that it was important that he be seen around the office, and he didn't want his assistant thinking that she was just a gofer. As he poured his cup, one of his new agents, Melissa Anderson (he was surprised that he remembered her name, having just met her for a few minutes the previous week) stopped and said hello. "You wouldn't know this, but I'm a speed reader, and one of the things I routinely do is scan through the various daily tip lists from around the country. This morning there was a blurb in the New Orleans' report about some shrimper smuggling a big fish box into southern Louisiana."

Bill's internal radar went off. "Very interesting, and a great catch. Do you know anyone in the New Orleans office?"

"Yep, there is a guy assigned there that was in my class at Quantico."

Bill could have followed up himself, but this agent had found something that might help Chicago with their case. "Call the guy, and see what else they know. Let me know what you find, and then follow up with a memo to everyone working on the Grant case. Great job finding that needle in the haystack." Melissa beamed, and headed back to her cubicle.

Ten minutes later she had just finished explaining to Bill about how the Marine recruit had played whistle blower, and about the pickup truck from Dallas, when Bill got an email marked "Urgent."

TO: Special Agent in Charge William Peterson
Chicago Office
FROM: Angela Robertson
Special Agent in Charge
New Orleans
CC: Assistant Director Arnold Cummins

Special Agent Peterson:

It has come to my attention that one of your agents directly contacted one of my agents about one of our cases here in Louisiana. I know you are new in your position, but you should be aware that protocol dictates that you contact me directly if you want information on a New Orleans case. In the future, please follow the correct SOP if you need to contact our office.

As for this case, this is about a small-time drug smuggler that was already on our radar, and you can rest assured that we will do our due diligence on this case when we have the resources to investigate. I'm sure you have your own case load to worry about, so please stay out of our cases.

Sincerely,

Angela

Bill winced. It wasn't so much that the New Orleans SAC had tried to put him in his place, but that she had also copied their immediate boss about his screw up. But at the same time, Bill had his mandate directly from their big boss. "Oh, well," he thought. "In for a penny…" He picked up his phone and asked his assistant, "Please see if you can get Randy Marshall in the Dallas office on the phone for me." Randy was Bill's counterpart in Dallas, and Bill had worked for Randy when Randy ran the Phoenix Office.

"Mr. Marshall on line one." Bill picked up the phone.

"Hey, Randy. How are things in Dallas?"

"Not bad. Congrats on your new gig. You deserve the opportunity. I don't have much time, so tell me why you are calling."

Bill got right to the point. He knew about time constraints. "Got a case that might, and I emphasize might, involve both our offices. Have you heard about our case where the police chief got shot by a couple of possible terrorists, and then the CSI team found radioactivity?"

"Yeah, read the case synopsis. How might we be involved in Dallas?"

Bill jumped back in before Randy could lose interest. "We tracked the pickup the suspects were using back to Chicago. The owner is a radicalized Islam convert that was already on our radar, but now he has disappeared. We think they somehow smuggled in a bomb in an oversized fish box, and then used welding equipment to somehow modify or disguise the bomb.

One of my sharp agents found a report from New Orleans about a very similar operation, where an oversized fish box was smuggled in, and picked up by a truck bearing a logo from Stan's Welding in Dallas. So, we have fish boxes and welders involved in both situations - and you know what we both have coming up in a couple of months."

Now Randy sounded more interested. "Conventions. The Secret Service has already taken over an entire floor here in the Federal Building in downtown Dallas. And this is too many coincidences for us not to check it out. Give me what else you have, and I'll get someone to check out this Stan's Welding.

Bill told Randy about the welder's truck, how Melissa Anderson had found the connection, and about the nasty email Bill had received from the New Orleans ASAC after Melissa had followed up for more info. Randy laughed. "Yep, the dragon lady in New

Orleans is well known for being pretty protective of her turf. But don't forget what your agent did. If this turns out to be a second bomb, you need to put Anderson in for an award for putting this together. I'll get back to you as soon as we can check things on our end. And for now, I suggest we just leave New Orleans out of the loop."

They said their goodbyes, and Bill felt a little better. The more people working a case, the better the odds that someone would find the clue that would break the case. But then he remembered his personnel problem, and knew he couldn't delay facing the issue any longer.

He called Chet Kingsley, and asked Chet to step over to Bill's office. Chet came in with a questioning look on his face, but turned serious when Bill said, "Close the door and sit down."

Chet sat in one of the chairs in front of Bill's desk, and Bill didn't waste any time on pleasantries. "I have an email from the Bureau of Ethical Responsibility stating that they show you maxing out your credit limit on your government American Express travel card, pulling cash advances at the Ameristar

Casino this past weekend. Anything you want to tell me?"

Chet just hung his head. Bill continued, "It has to be a gambling addiction, drugs, or somehow you have gotten into debt over your head. Which is it?"

Chet finally looked up at Bill. "I've gotten hooked on prescription opioids, mostly using OxyContin, because of my back pain issues. I've gotten pretty good at doctor shopping and getting prescriptions, but I've maxed out every credit card I have trying to buy the pills. I've tried going cold turkey, and even thought about voluntarily going into rehab. I can't beat this on my own. The good news is that I won enough money at the casino to pay back my credit cards, but I can't keep going on like this."

Bill thought for a moment. "I don't want to lose you as an agent, but you are going to have to go through rehab, and then face the Ethics Board. I can't guarantee what that result will be, but a successful stay in rehab will help. I have to place you on suspension, but I'm going to do so with pay. I want you to turn in your gun and badge now, and get yourself an appointment to see a PAR counselor this afternoon if possible. I want you in rehab by tomorrow. Let me know where you go, so that I can follow up and see how you are progressing."

Chet shook his head again. "Somehow I knew it would end up like this. I know you are new here, so do you want my suggestions on who should replace me as acting ASAC?"

Bill smiled at Chet still wanting to help. "I've been impressed by Melissa Anderson. What do you think of her?"

Chet thought for a moment, and then nodded. "She doesn't have much upper level management experience, but then, neither does anyone else in the office. She has led a couple of case teams, and done well in those assignments. She is sharp, but probably the only way to see if she is management material is to give her a chance."

Bill told him thanks for the input, and then held out his hand. Chet shook it, but Bill reminded him, "I still need your badge and gun. And remember to let me know by tomorrow where you are being admitted - what rehabilitation facility you have found. I wish you luck. I know that opioids are a tough addiction to beat, but I have faith you can do it. Let me know if there is anything I can do to help you or your family." Chet pulled off his shoulder holster, put it on Bill's desk, and pulled his credentials out of his wallet. "I feel naked without the gun, but losing the creds hurts more than turning in the firearm." Thanks for being so understanding - I know you could have fired me on the spot." Chet turned and walked out of the office.

Bill stared at the badge on his desk. The eagle with spread wings, over Lady Justice - Justicia - was a symbol of power combined with responsibility. Bill wondered if justice was being served in this case. Chet had hurt his back on the job, chasing down a fraudster that decided to try and run for it - and the drug addiction was a result of that original accident. But Bill was worried that the Bureau of Ethical Responsibility would not see things that way. Bill wanted to give Chet a second chance, but the Bureau was not big on second chances. Bill pulled Chet's pistol out of its holster, to make sure it wasn't loaded. "Cindy, can you come in here for a minute?"

"Yes, Boss?"

Please take Chet's badge and gun and bag them, and have them locked up in our property vault. I want to be the one to give them back to Chet when it is time to do so, so make sure they know down in property to take care of this stuff.

"Yes, Sir."

Bill sat for a moment with his eyes closed. Stressful confrontations were never fun, but they were a part of the job if you wanted to be the boss. The next part would be easier. He looked up and then dialed Melissa's extension. "Melissa, can you come up to my office for a moment?"

Chapter 6

Coincidentally, both the Hyatt in Chicago and the Omni in Dallas held their senior staff meetings at 9:00 on Tuesday mornings. Mondays were busy days at hotels, and Tuesdays just seemed to work better for meetings. Both hotels went through the usual agenda on vacancy rates, current and future promotions being run by the advertising people, major staffing issues, and complaints. Then they got down to the serious business of this summer's conventions.

In Chicago, hotel manager Lisa Brooks gave her staff a pep talk they probably didn't need. "You know this is our opportunity to shine before the world, with the hotel full of VIPs, and more important to us, reporters and television people that can provide us more good advertising than we could pay for in ten years - or just the opposite if we leave a bad impression on someone. We only have one chance to get this right, and we have to get it right. So, I'm going to ask that everyone cancel any vacation plans you have made until after the convention, unless it is absolutely vital. Does anyone have anything you absolutely have to take off for?" Her chief engineer, Steve Jennings, held up his hand. "Lisa, you know my daughter is getting married in two weeks up at Camp Newaygo in Michigan. I don't think I can get out of that one!" Everyone laughed. "We have a Friday night rehearsal, with the wedding on Saturday evening, followed by a reception. I can be back at work by Sunday evening, but I must have that Friday and Saturday off. All of you have received invitations to the wedding, but with the convention coming I'll understand if you want to skip the festivities. If you do want to come, there are plenty of rooms in the lodge and spaces in the cabins for everyone to stay at the camp. Just let me know by this evening, so that we can put you on or take you off the guest list."

Lisa interjected, "But if we want to come, we can drive up on Saturday, spend the night, and come back Sunday morning? How far is it?"

Steve smiled. "About three or four hours each way up 196. Let me know, and I'll get everyone a map that wants to attend."

Lisa looked around the room. Anyone else have any place they have to be over the next few weeks, or can I count on each of you to be here and helping to make this place the best hotel in the country?" Everyone laughed and applauded, and they ended their meeting.

At the Omni, the meeting took a similar turn. Joan Samuelson, one of the few female chief engineers in the hotel business around the country, told her boss that she needed the coming weekend off. "My daughter, Elizabeth, is graduating from UT Austin on Saturday afternoon, and I wouldn't miss that for all the conventions in the world."

Richard (Ricky to his friends) English told Joan that he absolutely understood, and for Joan to tell Liz congratulations from him and the hotel staff. Liz had worked summers at the hotel, so she was well known to most of the staff. Sally Billups, from Housekeeping, asked, "What is Liz planning on doing after graduation?"

Joan smiled. "Liz has accepted a job as a staff engineer at Exxon in Houston, making more than I do here at the hotel - not bad for a new college graduate. Her degree is in petroleum engineering, and apparently those people are in high demand. I had hoped she would relocate back here to Dallas or Ft. Worth, but Liz will be moving to Houston as soon as she gets through the graduation ceremonies." Joan added, "Liz' boyfriend is also moving to Houston, and I'm pretty sure that played a part in which job offer Liz accepted." Everyone around the table grinned. All of them had their own love stories, and some were even ongoing. Joan didn't think the guy was right for Liz, but she wasn't about to tell Liz (or Joan's hotel coworkers) anything about Liz' first true love - let Liz discover the guy's faults on her own. And it was a good job, even if it wasn't in Dallas.

Work schedules were printed and posted for the upcoming two weeks, and prying eyes at both hotels noted that the hotel facility managers would be missing for a few days. Both hotel engineers met with their own staffs, to pass on the information picked up at the executive staff meetings, and to make sure everyone knew their responsibilities while the chief engineers would be out of pocket. All major renovations at both facilities had been finished months ago, so there was nothing massive on the building agenda for either hotel - just the usual minor repair jobs that plague any large facility. All that work was assigned, and both engineers kept a list so that they could follow up on the repairs when they returned to work.

Chapter 7

Wednesday, May 20th

Randy Marshall called Bill Peterson back at 7:01 on Wednesday morning, just as Bill was arriving at the office. As usual, Randy jumped right to the point. "Operation Fish Box is getting more interesting by the minute. We sent a couple of agents out to Stan's Welding, out close to Plano, and our agents said the operation was already in an uproar. Stan's is about a twenty-person operation, with a dozen certified welders on staff. They operate a small fleet of blue trucks, going all over the Metroplex for welding jobs. They mostly do minor repairs, but recently they have gotten a couple of fairly large construction contracts, working on new apartments being built. So, they started expanding, hiring new welders. This past Saturday, everyone was at a job at a new complex going up in Rowlett. They all worked twelve hours, and then everyone just dumped their stuff back at the office and they all went out for a beer. On Monday, when they got back to the office, they discovered that one of their trucks was missing. They checked the job site, found that the truck was not there, and called the cops about the stolen truck.

Stan says he can't prove it, but he strongly suspects that the truck was taken by Brady Worthington. Worthington was one of the new welders hired to help with the increase in jobs, but Stan had to fire him just a few days later because of Worthington's racist comments toward his coworkers. About half of Stan's staff are either Hispanic or black. Stan was saying that Worthington was refusing to go on jobs with any of the minority welders, and was constantly making comments about their heritage, work habits, and even cleanliness. Stan said he wouldn't put up with that language from anyone, and told Worthington to hit the road about a week ago. Stan says it would have been pretty easy for Worthington to make duplicate keys for the stolen Ford pickup.

Here is where it gets interesting. We have a thick file on Mr. Worthington. He is a known member of several far-right wing militia groups here in Texas, including one called "Secede or Die," which advocates either killing or kicking all the minorities out of the state. He also matches the description the kid gave of one of the guys picking up the fish box in Louisiana.

The big question then is, what the hell is going on? You have allegedly Middle Eastern terrorists shooting a cop, and I've got far right nuts here in Texas with a second bomb? How does that compute?"

Bill Peterson thought for a moment. "Either we are way off on what we have been thinking, or else this is an extremely complicated plot by some major foreign player. I don't know any group that would use both Middle Eastern types and right-wing types in the same operation. We've got to be missing a big piece of the pie. Any idea where Worthington is holed up?"

Randy nodded, but Bill couldn't see that over the phone. "We have a pretty good idea of the hidey holes for the right-wing nuts - mostly small ranches outside of the major metropolitan areas of the state. We're watching a couple of them closely for any sign of Worthington. We're also reviewing results from highway cameras over that weekend, trying to track where the truck went when it came back from Louisiana. What have you developed on your suspects?"

Bill pulled a report from his desk. "As I mentioned to you earlier this week, we know the owner of the pickup involved in the shooting, but can't find him. We're pretty sure he is hiding somewhere here in the Chicago area, since this is his hometown. With some luck, we'll find him and his bomb before he can do any major damage. I've got some ideas on how to locate him, and I'll keep you informed as we make progress. Any thoughts on why the bombers need welders? What could they be welding that would keep us from finding something that is highly radioactive?"

"Maybe some sort of shield to hide the radioactivity? Maybe welding the bomb into a shape that looks like something ordinary, so that we will walk right by it when we do our inspections?" Randy was just throwing out ideas, but Bill understood. Sometimes something good comes from just brainstorming.

Bill asked, "Do we want to get a bigger group looking at this? Do we have enough concrete evidence to convince the powers that be in D.C. that we are on the right track? I'm having to send daily reports to the Director, but he has yet to either say, "Keep going" or "Start over." I don't know how he feels about the progress, or lack of progress, on this case. Do you know him very well? Any thoughts on how we should proceed?"

Randy cut Bill off. "You don't have to worry about the Director, as long as he keeps quiet. When you need to worry is when he starts making suggestions about your case. Right now, he is reading your reports, along with a thousand other reports every day. As long as you don't screw up and get half of Chicago blown into the lake, you are doing fine as far as he is concerned."

Bill laughed a little at that. "Thanks for the vote of confidence, if that is what you meant. I'll let you know if we develop anything else on our suspect, or if I find the bomb in the basement of the Federal Building here in the Windy City." They hung up and got back to work.

Chapter 8

Thursday, May 21st

Bill and Melissa were going over the latest on Abriz Mohammed, the listed owner of the pickup they suspected had been in on the Michigan operation. Mohammed lived in a row house on the south side of Chicago, close to West Rogers Park. He (and his pickup) were nowhere to be found, but interviews with his neighbors had gotten the FBI a list of his friends, and the fact that he attended Jama Masjid, the mosque on Maplewood Avenue not far from Mohammed's home. They had agents watching the homes of several of Mohammed's friends, but no sign of him at those locations, either. So, Bill Peterson decided to call in a favor.

About five years ago, when Bill was working out of the Phoenix FBI office, he had led a task force called Operation Ecstasy. Phoenix had gotten word that several young women had been slipped MDMA (street name - Ecstasy) while drinking at bars close to the University of Arizona in Tucson. They reported to the police that they had been molested, but had no idea what had happened to them after they started drinking, or who had doctored their drinks. After blood tests showed MDMA in their bloodstreams, the FBI was contacted for help.

Bill and his team set up hidden cameras in a couple of cooperating bars on the main drag near campus, and watched the partying in real time, as well as recording everything on tape, from a van parked out on the street. When they got lucky and caught two guys slipping powder into a couple of girls' drinks, they arrested the guys and kept the girls from drinking the spiked alcohol. The guys admitted to being members of a UA fraternity that thought it was "fun" to use Ecstasy on their potential victims. The perps quickly turned, identifying the dealer that had been selling them the drugs, and when he was arrested, he gave up the Mexican gang in San Diego that had been his supplier. Bill and his team wrapped up the entire drug chain, and shut down the operation before any more coeds could be attacked. The University expelled some of the frat members, and banned the fraternity from all campus activities for a year.

It turned out that one of the intended victims the night of the arrests was 21-year-old Cheryl Simpson, the daughter of the Phoenix Chief of Police, Glenn Simpson. When Glenn heard about Bill's team stopping the Ecstasy users from getting to his daughter, he called Bill, and told him, "I owe you a big one. Anytime, anywhere - you just let me know, and I'll do whatever I can to repay you. Maybe one day you'll have a daughter, and understand what it is like to send her out into the world. I always worried that something might happen to her down in Tucson. I knew we had raised her right, but you can't always control outside influences. When you turn them loose, all you can do is pray - and you were the answer to my prayers."

Bill thanked Glenn for the kind words, and said something about "Just doing my job." But he knew he had saved that girl and others, and there was a level of intrinsic satisfaction and pride that helped to keep him going on days when things weren't going that well. And Bill filed away that offer of help from the Phoenix police chief. Sometimes police forces and the FBI didn't see eye to eye, so it was nice to have an extra arrow in the quiver if needed. Over time Bill and Glenn got to be pretty good friends, with the two of them going out with their wives several times a year. Glenn looked at Bill as the son he never had, and Glenn tried to serve as a mentor to the young FBI agent.

Now Glenn Simpson was the Chief of Police in Chicago, having moved to the bigger job about a year before Bill got his new position. Bill knew the FBI didn't have any undercover operatives in the Jama Masjid mosque, but he was hoping that Simpson would have someone in the mosque, and that Simpson would be willing to use his undercover operative to help find information on where Abriz Mohammed might be hiding. Peterson had a hunch that someone from the mosque was covering for Mohammed. Whether that person knew what Mohammed was planning was a different story - it could be that Mohammed had just told his helper that he needed to lay low for a while, and any Muslim is taught that providing hospitality is a requirement handed down from Allah.

Bill called Chief Simpson. He couldn't get Simpson on the phone - of course he was in a meeting - but Bill left a message, and twenty minutes later Simpson returned the phone call.

"Hey, Bill. Welcome to Chicago. Glad to see you got the promotion. How does Julie like the place so far?"

"She's still unpacking, and getting to know her way around town. It will take some time, but she'll get comfortable. How is your daughter doing?"

"She is wonderful, thanks in part to what you did to help save her. She is an elementary school teacher in Phoenix. She got married about two years ago, to a really nice guy, and they have a baby on the way. I'm going to be a grandfather!"

"Good to hear, Glenn. Listen, I've got a case that could impact both of us, and we probably need to get together to discuss it. Unfortunately, there are some security concerns, so I don't want a big meeting with both of our staffs involved - too much of a chance of leaks. Can you meet me for lunch?

Or a beer after work? I really want to talk to you about this situation, and it needs to be just you and I."

"My schedule is packed for today. How about lunch tomorrow? I'm a member at the Union League Club over on Jackson. I'll treat, and if you like the place I'll even nominate you for a membership. Meet you there at, say, 12:30? Just give them my name at the front desk."

Bill quickly glanced at his schedule. He would have to rearrange a meeting, but getting with Glenn was important. "OK, Glenn, 12:30 tomorrow will be fine. And, again, just you and me - we need to play this one close to the vest."

"Alright, Bill, I'll defer to your judgment on this one. My staff will know who I'm meeting for lunch, and people will talk - so be prepared for that."

"Thanks again, Glenn. See you tomorrow."

Chapter 9

Friday, May 22nd

At 12:25 that afternoon Bill Peterson gave his name to the head porter at the Union League, and he was led to Glenn Simpson's table. Glenn stood up as Bill arrived, and they shook hands.

"What do you think of our little club?" Glenn started. "I can put you up for membership, but, unfortunately, it takes two members for a nomination. I'm not sure we can dig up somebody willing to let in an FBI guy. Do you still have access to Hoover's old files? Maybe we can blackmail somebody into vouching for you."

Bill just shook his head. "Yes, you have a great place here. It's unfortunate that it will probably just be a smoking pile of radioactive rubble in another couple of months."

Glenn looked at him long and hard. "I think you are serious. Tell me what's going on."

"You remember that police chief that got shot up in Michigan a couple of weeks ago?

We think those guys were terrorists, bringing in a bomb, to use on the Republican Convention here in July. We found the container they used to transport the bomb into the U.S., and our techs say the foam indentations show a bomb weighing close to a half ton. Something that big will level about eight square blocks of Chicago, centered on the McCormick Convention Center, or wherever they place the bomb. Another 20 square blocks will probably be uninhabitable for about 100 years, due to the radioactivity scattered by the bomb. We think they have an RDD, and not an actual atomic or hydrogen bomb. We traced the terrorist's pickup truck back to Chicago, but we haven't had any luck finding the bad guys, the bomb, or the pickup. So, I need your help.

But one thing I have to do is swear you to secrecy. If word gets out that we are looking for an RDD, panic will ensue, and the terrorists may decide to cut their losses and go ahead and set off the bomb. So that is why I asked for us to meet privately. Years ago, you told me that if I ever needed a favor to come see you. I'm calling in that chit now.

I don't want you telling your staff, the mayor, or anyone else about this conversation. There are too many possibilities of leaks. We're lucky nothing has gotten out so far since the incident up in Michigan."

Glenn set back in his chair, stunned. "Damn. I know you said this was important, but I wasn't expecting something like this. For right now, I'll go with your plan of not telling anyone - but I reserve the right to change my mind as we get closer to the convention, if we haven't found these critters and their bomb. I agree we need to search quietly. What can the Chicago Police Department do to help you find these guys?"

"We've tracked the pickup's owner, Abriz Mohammed, back to a Southside address, and we've quietly interviewed his neighbors. They tell me he attends the Jama Masjid, a mosque on Maplewood. I'm hoping you have someone undercover in that mosque, who can get us info on where we might can find this guy. We need to know who he hangs out with, and, more importantly, where they might be hiding. I don't want to burn your guy, assuming you have a guy there, but this is important. How can we set something up where I can talk to your undercover operative? And is there a way to do that where he can stay undiscovered?"

Glenn thought for a moment. "We have people in just about every mosque in town, just keeping low and listening for rumbles. We haven't heard about anything big going down, so your guys may be avoiding spreading rumors - which speaks to professionalism. Let me make a phone call to my Operations Deputy, and we'll see how we can set up a meet.

As for right now, this place makes a great Trout Almandine for lunch. I suggest we enjoy lunch here while we still can!"

Bill grinned, and looked down at his menu. Maybe there was a way out of this mess after all.

Chapter 10

Later that afternoon, just as Bill and Glenn were finishing their lunch, a plumbing truck backed up to the loading dock at the Hyatt Regency McCormick Place. There was an intercom button by the loading dock door, and the truck's driver pushed the button.

"Yes, can we help you?"

"I have a delivery for Steve Jennings, your engineer."

"Mr. Jennings is out of the office today. Can you bring the stuff back on Monday?"

"Yes, but this thing is heavy. We would have to charge you an extra $200 for the redelivery. I have three guys here to help me get this to - he looked down at his clipboard and notes, in case he was on camera - room B 144. Can you get someone to let us in? Please?"

There as a pause, as if the operator was thinking. "Okay, I'll get someone from housekeeping to come down and let you in, and show you the way to that storeroom. You will have to sign in on the clipboard hanging next to the door where you are standing, and you will have to sign back out when you leave, showing the time you left. You can leave a copy of your invoice with the person sent down to let you in. Any questions?"

"Thanks! It is Friday afternoon, and this is our last delivery. We appreciate your cooperation."

Thirty minutes later the water heater was in the storeroom, sitting next to two other spares that looked identical to the one they had just delivered. It took all four guys to maneuver the water heater into the freight elevator, down a couple of levels, and then through the halls to the storeroom. The final battery was quickly added, and the bomb was armed.

They arranged the heaters so that you could not tell which was the oldest, and which was the newest. The sign-in log was completed with a scrawled, unreadable signature. But that didn't matter, as the logs were never reviewed, anyway. And the housekeeping employee sent to show the way to the storeroom made sure that the "invoice" never made it to Steve Jennings's mailbox. By Monday, no one would remember that a delivery had come in while Steve was at his daughter's wedding.

In Dallas, the bomb delivery procedure was very similar. This time the dock was under the ballrooms attached to the Omni, and the delivery truck had to wait until a UPS truck moved away from the loading dock to free up a space. The guy running the loading dock that afternoon was a cousin to the truck's driver, and the guard had made sure he had the dock assignment when the water heater was being delivered. At the dock, another friend met the truck, and helped the guys in plumbing outfits and cowboy boots to get their water heater into the storeroom in the bowels of the hotel. No record was made of that delivery at all.

One thing that was an issue at the Omni was that the Omni used AO Smith commercial water heaters, and not the ones made by Rheem. That was one reason they had to sneak in the delivery, instead of just saying that they were adding to the hotel's inventory of spare heaters. The delivery team had to hide the Rheem heater behind the spare AO Smith water heaters, and hope that the discrepancy would not be found before it was time to explode their bomb. They laid their water heater on its side, and covered it with some PVC piping they found in the storeroom. Unless you were really looking, the addition to the storeroom would not be noticed at all. Again, draft emails were prepared, and then read later and erased by a North Korean covert operator assigned to the DPRK embassy in Stockholm. In North Korea, the Supreme Leader wanted to throw a party based on the success of the mission, but General Shin cautioned that there was still much to be done before the mission could be called a success.

By dusk on Friday the Chicago group was at their prayers, while the Dallas team was sitting at a table in a bar where the exotic dancers were just starting to warm up. That team was already on their second round of beers. Two different groups with different philosophies and beliefs, with the same goal in mind - the total disruption of the United States' political landscape.

Chapter 11

Monday, May 25th

Memorial Day

Bill was in his office on Monday morning, as usual (holidays don't count when the fate of your city is in your hands), when he got two quick phone calls. The first was from Randy Marshall in Dallas. "Hey, Bill. Just to keep you up to date, we raided a ranch outside of Forney, Texas yesterday afternoon. Based on our camera work tracking the Stan's Welding pickup and a couple of tips, we had enough information to go for a search warrant with a friendly judge here in town.

The place was deserted, but we did find the Stan's Welding pickup in the barn, and an empty fish box, just like the one you described finding up in Michigan. Both registered high on a Geiger counter. So now we have more proof that there are two bombs out there, if not more. When this report hits headquarters, we are going to be inundated with people trying to tell us how to do our jobs, just so that they can play CYA if the shit hits the fan and one or more of these bombs ends up going off this summer. I know you are fairly new at the job, so I thought I better warn you about what's coming. You'll have everyone from the Secret Service and Homeland Security to the Firearms people breathing down your neck in short order. And when it starts getting political, there is a much greater chance of something leaking out about the potential bombs.

I've already called the Director, and asked him to run what interference he can for us - he works for the Attorney General, and they can go to the President if necessary - but I don't know how long they can hold off the thundering herd. So, our timeline for finding the bombs just got a lot shorter, or else we will be bogged down in so many meetings to discuss what we should or should not be doing that we will never get the chance to get any actual work done.

Anyway, tell your agent Anderson that she done good. Without her getting a sniff of this second bomb, we would still be way behind the curve. And maybe this news will get our lady friend down in New Orleans off her ass, and she'll take a closer look at that shrimp boat. Maybe we can backtrack to whoever sent these things toward the United States."

Bill said, "Thanks for the heads up. And back tracking is a good idea. I'll get more people trying to figure out where our bomb came across the border, too. I think you and I ought to start talking at least every couple of days, so that we can keep up with what we've found on each end of this nightmare. I can call you, or you call me, first thing in the morning until we get this solved."

They both agreed to talk regularly, said their goodbyes, and went back to work.

Bill's second phone call was from his buddy at the Chicago Police Department, Chief Simpson. Glenn started off quietly. "You alone in your office?"

"Yes."

"Okay, we've set up a meet for you with our undercover guy from the Jama Masjid. Tonight at 9:00, you will be picked up at your house by one of our confiscated drug dealer cars, so that it will not look like a police car. When the car stops at your place you need to be ready, and jump in the back seat. You will be taken to a condemned row of tenement houses out close to where our suspect lives. You need to wear dark clothing, and come armed, just in case.   You will be let out at the condemned buildings about 9:30, and you are to make your way to the second floor of the building on the north end of the row. Supposedly no one is crashing there, so you should be alone. Our guy will find you there, and you will have about fifteen minutes to talk. He already knows who you are looking for, so if he has any updated info on Mohammed he'll pass it on.

   You need to let him leave, and then about 10:00 our car will again come by and pick you up out in front of the tenement. You will be home by 10:30 or so. Obviously, no one can know about the meet. And we can probably just do this one time without burning our source. It was difficult to set this up on short notice, and we don't want to raise suspicions about our guy in the mosque. You got all of that?"

   Bill told Glenn, "Yep, got it. And thanks, Glenn. This pays me back for what we did in Tucson. And now I'll owe you one, so call me if the FBI can do something to help out the Chicago police force. And, hopefully, this will help us to save the Union League building - so if you can find a second person to nominate me for membership, the next lunch there will be on my tab."

Glenn laughed. "You got a deal. Now catch these critters, and keep that bomb from knocking half of downtown Chicago into the lake."

Chapter 12

Julie, Bill's wife, noticed how jumpy he was that evening. He told her he was going to meet with an undercover operative that worked for the Chicago Police Department, but he wouldn't give her any details. So, she got worried, because he was so nervous.

He tried to watch a little television, but could not get interested in anything. At 8:57, he kissed Julie, told her, "I'll be careful. Should be home by midnight or a little later," and walked down the sidewalk toward the street in front of their new house. The car was right on time, but when Bill started to get in the back seat he noticed that the car's interior light was not working. One of the officers in the front said, "Yep, we disabled the light. No need to advertise when we let you off." They headed for the south side of Chicago. There was still a lot of traffic on the roads, even that late - but the driver knew where he was going, and they made pretty good time.

The guy in the front passenger seat turned around to look at Bill. "Well, you won't pass as a gangbanger, but maybe no one will notice you until you can get in the building. They told you second floor, north end?" Bill nodded, not trusting himself to speak. The guy in the front seat continued. "When you get out of the car, step immediately into the shadow of the building. Then wait a minute, to let your eyes adjust. Do NOT, under any circumstances, use a flashlight. This has to be done completely using moonlight and what little ambient lighting there will be at the scene. So be careful going up the stairs to the second floor - test each step before you take it, and watch for missing treads, and then holes in the floor when you get to the second story. If you can see well enough, once you get to the second floor, get away from the stairs, and over to the wall by the street side of the building. Stay away from any windows - we don't want shadows moving that could be seen from the street.

The guy you will be meeting will go by the name, 'Jim.' Let him come to you. It might take him a few minutes, because he must make sure he is not being followed, and that there isn't any interest in you after you go into the building. Let me see your cell phone."

Bill handed over his phone, and the cop put a number into the phone. He handed it back to Bill in the backseat. "Okay, the contact is listed as 'PD.' When Jim leaves, wait five minutes, and then call us. Just say, "Go," and then hang up. We will drive by about three minutes later. If you get downstairs and don't see our car, just wait in the shadows until you see us approaching. Don't run to the car, but don't be slow about it, either. I know the Chief told you to come armed, but try not to shoot anybody - the paperwork would take all night, and we would like to get home to our families at a reasonable hour, too. You got all of that?"

Bill said, "Got it." He put the phone back into his back pocket, and again started looking at the bleak neighborhoods they were driving through. There wasn't much traffic in this part of town, and not many people out on the streets, either. What streetlights there were had been shot out, so it was a pretty dark ride, except for when they went by a bar or laundromat with a neon sign glowing out front. Those stood out like islands on a dark sea.

The guy in the front seat turned to face Bill one more time. "Okay, get ready. We had a patrol car go through this street about ten minutes ago, and he didn't see anything. We can't afford a drive by - it might attract too much attention if we came by twice - so this has to work the first time. We will slow to a crawl, but not stop completely - so be prepared for a little movement when you hit the street. Here we go!"

The car made a right turn and started slowing. When they were nearly stopped, the guy in the front said, "Go!" and Bill opened his door and stepped out, finding his footing easily. By the time he got out of the car he was closer to the second building in the row, instead of the one on the end that he wanted, but he quickly moved into the shadow of that building. After giving his eyes a minute to get used to the dark, he slowly started moving back toward the entrance of the north building. The door had been barricaded, but the wooden bars across the door had been peeled back by someone who really wanted to get into the place, and the door stood about half open. Bill slipped inside, happy to be off the street, but wondering what he might encounter inside the building. He knew there would be rats, but he hoped to only see the four-legged kind. He again stood still for a minute, listening for any sounds from the street and inside the building, but he didn't hear anything.

There was a bank of mailboxes on the wall by the door, ripped off the wall, and then Bill could see the beginning of the stairway past the mailboxes. He carefully picked his way to the stairs, and slowly started heading up. The good news is that there was a stair rail, and that helped him to test each stair, and helped to guide him when the stairway made a turn halfway between the floors.

It did not take Bill long to reach the second floor, even though it seemed like forever with all his senses on high alert. He could smell left over fires and cooking smells, and the odor of marijuana hung heavily in the air. The floor felt gritty beneath his feet, but he wasn't about to sit down. He moved over to the street wall, trying to stay away from the windows as requested. He found an area where the sheetrock had been ripped from the wall, and he stood next to an exposed stud, using that as support. He wasn't known for his patience, but he could wait when he had to - and here he didn't have much of a choice.

Again, it seemed like forever, but it was probably only a few minutes before he felt another presence coming into the room. "Jim?" he called softly. The other guy just whispered, "Shhh. Just give me another minute." Bill waited while the other guy made sure they were alone.

Jim finally walked over within about six feet of Bill. "Okay, this is probably close enough that we can talk softly, but far enough that you can't see my face. I don't want you to be able to identify me if we were to meet under different circumstances sometime in the future. Let me get right to the point, because we may not have much time here. I know what you are looking for, and who you are trying to find, so you don't have to waste any time briefing me.

Abriz Mohammed hangs out with a guy named Hamid Youssef. That's not their real names, but what they started using when they got "converted" to Islam while in Joliet for armed robbery. The Chief should be able to give you files on both of them. Surprisingly, they have still been coming by the mosque about once a week or so. The interesting thing is that they have been bringing two newcomers with them that I swear are not native to Chicago, or even the United States. Just something about the way they act makes me think they are foreign. Those may be the terrorists that helped to bring in the bomb. Youssef's mom has a place on Delaware Street. Her name is Delores Madison. Another interesting coincidence is that her place has an attached garage. So, you might can find all of these suspects at that address, plus their pickup. They haven't been driving the pickup to the mosque, or I would have spotted it - so they must have at least one additional vehicle. If you can get a team in place before you raid that house, you can probably identify that second vehicle, too.

That's about all I can give you about those two. If you had asked me, I wouldn't have picked them out as being radical enough to get in bed with some terrorists, but I have been known to be wrong about people before. That's why I'm no longer married. You got any quick questions before I disappear?"

Bill just said, "Thanks for your help. I know getting this set up was difficult for you, and I appreciate the effort you made to get here and get your information to me. You may have helped to save thousands of lives, and half of Chicago."

Jim nodded, but Bill couldn't see it. Jim faded back into the darkness, going as quietly as he had come. Bill waited the necessary five minutes, even though he wanted to make the call as soon as Jim walked back into the shadows. Bill didn't have to say anything - the guy on the other end of the phone said, "On the way." as soon as he answered the call. Bill headed back down the stairs, again trying to stay as quiet as possible. The timing was good. Bill walked out the door of the building just as the car turned onto their street. Bill quickly got to the car and jumped in the back seat, and they were on their way out of the neighborhood - hopefully with no one noticing that they had been there. Bill was back home by 11:00, with Julie meeting him at the door with a big hug.

Bill stayed up until after midnight, writing his notes about what he had learned, with a copy to his team and the Director in D.C. He tried to get a few hours of sleep, but he was still pretty keyed up from the meet, and didn't feel like himself when he got up on Tuesday morning.

Chapter 13

Tuesday, May 26th

Bill still had about a half cup of his Starbuck's double espresso when he got to his office suite. He normally didn't drink that strong a cup of coffee, but that morning he needed it. He was intercepted outside his reception area by Melissa Anderson. She handed him a copy of the Chicago Sun-Times, and said, "Two pieces of bad news. The first is the headline in the paper."

Bill glanced down at the newspaper to see in a big, bold type: TERRORISTS MAY HAVE ATOMIC BOMB IN CHICAGO. The subheading was almost as bad: HOMELAND SECURITY TO LEAD SEARCH FOR BOMB. Melissa added, "And to top things off, a lady from Homeland Security is waiting in your office. She refused to wait out in the waiting area, insisting that we let her in to your office, and said she wanted to see everything we have on our bomb search. We've stalled her so far on that request. Good luck with this one!" She started to walk back to her office, but Bill stopped her. "Come on into my office with me. I'm not sure how I'm going to handle this, but I will most certainly want you as a witness." Melissa grinned. "I thought this might get interesting." She followed Bill into his inner office.

A fortyish lady was sitting behind Bill's desk, drumming her fingers on his calendar pad. Bill tried to start the conversation off on a civil tone. "Hello. I'm Bill Peterson, the Agent in Charge of this office. May I help you?"

The lady stood, fished in her purse for a card, and handed it to Bill. "I'm Jackie Kirksey, Under Secretary for Terrorism at the Department of Homeland Security. I will be taking over your search for the terrorists and their bomb."

Bill asked, rather calmly he thought, "Okay, you are welcome to it. Just let me see what you have in writing from the FBI Director relieving me of my responsibilities in this case. Or do you have something from the Attorney General, or the President? Otherwise, by law, this is still my case. I'm not going to turn everything over to you on just your word. If you don't have anything in writing, then let's get on the phone and see if we can get this straightened out right now."

The lady just stared at Bill. "You are not going to take me at my word? I'm an Under Secretary at the umbrella organization that handles ALL the security for this country. If I say this is my investigation, then this is my investigation."

Bill just shook his head. "Nope. I don't know if you are a lawyer, like I am, but the law is clear in this regard. Unless you have something from someone higher up the food chain, we are staying at status quo ante. I'll be happy to get Melissa here to give you a briefing on where we stand, and any suggestions you may have on how to improve on what we are doing would be welcome. But understand that they would just be suggestions, not orders. Is that clear?"

Bill continued, before Jackie could reply. "What did you do? Go to your boss and suggest you come here and try and take over this investigation from the new rookie Agent in Charge?" Jackie flushed. Bill jumped on her again. "That's what I thought. And one more thing. Give me your phone."

Jackie bristled. "Why would I do that?"
Bill smiled. "Obviously you missed the sign
on the door downstairs that once you enter
the Federal Building all personal property is
subject to search and seizure. Now give me
your phone, or else I'll get your boss on the
line right now." Jackie flushed again, but
fished in her purse and handed Bill her
phone. "And the password?" She gave him
her PIN, and Bill typed it in. "Okay, Melissa,
get on your phone, and give me the number
for the Chicago Sun-Times. There are several
calls here last night to Chicago Area Codes,
and I bet not all of them were about getting
hotel reservations."

Melissa did a quick search, and read out
the Chicago Sun-Times mail switchboard
number to Bill. "Yep, just what I thought.
Ms. Kirksey, you called the paper a couple of
times, and you are most certainly the source
of today's headlines. We could probably
prove that quickly, because the paper records
all their incoming calls. When you told them
about the bomb, you violated the National
Secrecy Act, and that call is also a violation of
the oath you took when you got your security
clearance.

I now have a couple of choices. I can arrest you for breaking the law, or I can ask for your resignation as Under Secretary. I don't really want to arrest you, because that would mean more publicity about the alleged bomb, and it would look bad for both of our agencies. Your call."

Jackie sputtered, "You can't do that!"

Bill looked at Melissa. "You still have your Miranda Card? Read Ms. Kirksey her rights and then put her in cuffs."

Melinda started off from memory. "You have the right to remain silent," but she was quickly interrupted by Jackie Kirksey. "Okay, I'll resign when I get back to Washington."

Bill held up his hand. "Nope. Not good enough." He hit the button on his phone that connected him to his administrative assistant, Cindy Wade, sitting in the outer office. "Cindy, please take this down, type it up for me, and bring it into my office as soon as you get it done. 'I, Jackie Kirksey, Under Secretary for Terrorism in the United States Department of Homeland Security, do hereby resign my position, effective immediately.' Please date it today with a time on it five minutes from now. I apologize for the short notice, but this is important."

Cindy said, "Right away, sir." Five minutes later she was in his office with the typewritten resignation. She looked at Bill, Jackie, and Melissa, with questions in her eyes, but she knew if they wanted her to know what was going on they would fill her in later.

Bill said, "Thanks, Cindy. You can stay for this part, so that I've got a second witness. Ms. Kirksey, either you sign the resignation, or you will be led out of here in handcuffs. I know when you get back to your office you will claim to your boss that you were forced to sign under duress, and that is why I wanted two witnesses to your signature. A report detailing this entire matter will be made to the FBI Director, and he may still decide to press charges against you. What you did was not only a violation of the law, but totally unethical, and it may result in panic in the streets of Chicago. Now sign the form, go back to your hotel and check out, and go straight to O'Hare. You should still be able to catch a flight back to D.C. before noon. If I find you in Chicago after 3:00 this afternoon, I will have you arrested, resignation or not. Is that understood?"

Jackie Kirksey walked to Bill's desk, picked up a pen, and signed the form. She started to take it with her, but Bill stopped her. "Nope, that stays with us." She tossed the signed form back on Bill's desk, and stormed out of the office, not looking at anyone.

After she slammed the door to the outer office, Melissa started to applaud, quickly joined by Cindy. Bill just shook his head. "Okay, you two, I want you to countersign the resignation as witnesses, and then get out. I've got to make a lot of phone calls quickly, explaining what just happened, and trying to get us some help with the press. Any and all suggestions on how to handle the press will be greatly appreciated. Melissa, it would probably be a good idea to put a loose tail on Ms. Kirksey, to make sure she follows orders and goes back to Washington. Let me know if that situation goes south. Cindy, please get me the Director on the phone, if he is available." Both ladies headed out of Bill's office, grinning at one another. Bill started making notes of the meeting with Ms. Kirksey while the conversation was still fresh in his mind. He also needed to figure out a way to explain to the FBI Director what had just happened, and why. It was going to be a long morning, and he hadn't even started thinking about the information he had gotten from the Chicago Police's undercover operative on Monday night.

The Director was not only agreeable to Bill's suggestions, but actually laughed when Bill told him how they had come close to putting the lady from Homeland Security under arrest. The Director told Bill, "I'll have to think about how to handle that one. This may be one we put on the shelf, to be pulled down and used when needed. I'll make sure she doesn't get her old job back. That I can handle with a call to the Attorney General. As for the press, let us put out a press release from this office. We have people that are good at that sort of thing, and we don't need you getting tripped up by some fast-talking reporter. You just keep saying something like, "We don't comment on ongoing investigations, if there is such an investigation.' The best bet is to avoid the reporters if you can, but if you get stopped, just keep repeating, 'no comment."

Bill thanked the Director for his help, and then called in his immediate staff. He filled them in on what he had learned on Monday night from the undercover operative, without revealing his source. They all understood about protecting sources. A plan was developed to surveil the house where they thought the terrorists might be staying, with round the clock coverage. As it turned out, there was an apartment for rent across the street from Mrs. Madison's place on Delaware, so an agent was sent to see the real estate firm that was handling that rental. The idea was for the FBI to pay the rent on the vacant apartment for a month, but to move people in surreptitiously. By coming in the back entrance of the complex, and keeping all the lights off in the apartment, they hoped to set up an observation post without anyone knowing they were there. The rental firm was just happy to get the money, and agreed to quit showing the apartment for the next 30 days.

Bill told his staff, "I know you have all done surveillance before, so this is just a reminder. Any sort of light, movement behind the curtains, or anyone seen coming or going from the apartment will set off all sorts of alarms across the street, where they will already be paranoid. We probably have at best 48 hours before someone notices we are in that apartment. With some luck, we'll find our critters and wrap this up pretty quickly. This is our best chance, and probably our only chance, to get these guys before they explode their bomb. So, do it right, and let's make this work."

Everyone got their assignments, and the meeting broke up. Cindy brought in copies of the press release prepared by the public relations people at FBI Headquarters for everyone to read.

The headline in this morning's Chicago Sun-Times was factually incorrect. We know of NO atomic bomb in the hands of terrorists in the Chicago area, or anywhere else in the United States or the rest of the world.

With the Republican National Convention coming to town next month, that event makes the city a potential target for a terrorist event - just like a Super Bowl or any other major event that draws people from

around the country. The FBI is continually working with our sister agencies in law enforcement, including the Secret Service, Homeland Security, the Coast Guard, and the Chicago Police Department, to guard against possible terrorist attacks during the convention. We feel we have a good plan in place to avoid such attacks. While we cannot list all the security measures we will be taking to ensure the safety of our guests during the convention, you can rest assured that all possible precautions are being undertaken. Chicago can feel safe from terror before, during, and after the convention, thanks to the efforts of all our law enforcement teams.

Chapter 14

Bill called Randy Marshall in Dallas. "Hey, Randy. Lots going on, and I need to bring you up to date. I don't know if you have seen the Sun-Times headlines from this morning, but it turns out that a lady from Homeland Security tipped them off about the bomb. Of course, they got the story wrong, but that is par for the course for the press. More interestingly, she showed up in my office this morning, claiming she was taking over the investigation, which would now be under her agency. I called her bluff, and she folded. I then found out that she was the one that had tipped off the press, so I gave her a choice of resigning, or being placed under arrest. She chose to resign as Under Secretary.

Headquarters is putting out a press release claiming that there is no atomic bomb, and that we have security under control. I'll have my admin assistant email you a copy, in case anything hits the news in Texas.

We also got some credible information on where some of our critters may be in hiding, and we are setting up surveillance on that place as we speak. Hopefully that will result in some arrests shortly.

The bad news, besides not having located the bomb, is that our investigation of how the bomb was smuggled into the country has pretty much stalled. We tracked the pickup truck we had been watching up to Port Hope, Michigan, but no one is pointing a finger at another boat captain, saying, 'That's your smuggler.' Either they don't know who is doing it, or they are closing ranks and not finding any reasons to open up to law enforcement."

Randy was quiet for a moment. "I've got a wild hare idea. Have you checked to see which captains have a boat that is completely paid for? Those guys barely make enough to feed their families and make their boat payments. If someone has a clear title to their boat, that might show who is bringing in some extra cash under the table. You could check with the banks in that area, or maybe the Michigan Secretary of State's office can run some sort of check on boat titles in that part of the state. Just something to consider...."

Bill nearly leaped out of his chair. "Great idea. I'll get an agent working on that immediately. What have you learned about your right wingers?"

Randy sighed. "Not much new on this end. We are going back through our database of people with known connections, trying to find someone who might be hiding our critters. But it is about like the old 'Six Degrees of Kevin Bacon' game. Almost everyone in our database knows someone who knows someone who knows one of our targets. So, we are having problems cutting down our possibilities. If you have any ideas on how to help that process, let me know. In the meantime, we are pretty much just treading water. Bill told Randy, "Let me get our IT people talking to your IT people. Maybe our guys can think of some filters you haven't tried. The odds are against it, but it doesn't hurt to try."

Randy added, "One more thing. We did send people to New Orleans, to interview the boat captain that brought in our fish box. His contact is with one of the Mexican cartels, and they call him whenever they want him to make a smuggling run. He doesn't even know a real name. We've got the DEA and the CIA working on the Mexican end, to see what they can find, if anything."

Chapter 15

Wednesday, May 27th

A ten-man FBI SWAT team had flown into O'Hare on Tuesday night, ready to assist with the takedown of the house on Delaware. They checked in with Bill on Wednesday morning, and he told them to be ready, because he didn't know when they would have to move. They were given a conference room there at the Chicago FBI office, and started studying the satellite and Google Maps photos of the area around the house that they might have to assault. Bill picked two of his agents to liaison with the team, with the understanding that the team leader had carte blanche control of the takedown when it was initiated.

Things came to a head about 10:30 that morning, when Bill got a call from one of the agents on site at the observation point in the apartment across the street from the house being surveilled. "Boss, I think we're busted, and we're going to have to move in."

"What happened?"

"Some idiot real estate agent didn't read his morning notes, and brought a couple over to see this apartment. I'm afraid word is going to spread pretty quickly that something weird is going on in this place, and our chickens across the street are going to flee the coop."

"What can you tell me about who is in the house?"

"We have four adult males in the place for sure right now. Not sure about the fifth one - haven't seen Mohammed. We do have Youssef in the house, along with a couple of guys that match the description we got from that Michigan police chief. The garage door has been kept closed, so we don't know if the pickup is here or not. What do you want us to do?"

"Stand by. I'm going to get the SWAT team moving now. Stay where you are until after they take the place - I don't want you involved in that, because you are not wearing body armor and you don't have enough firepower. You can be oversight. I'll get the SWAT team your cell number, so that you can talk directly to them as to what you have seen. Let me know if anything changes, but

135

they should hit the place in about thirty minutes."

"10-4, boss. Tell 'um to make it quick."

Bill told the SWAT team leader what he had been told about the situation on Delaware. The team leader told Bill he wished he had more time to prepare, but that "not enough time to prepare" had been a standard complaint since George Washington's day. Bill laughed, and told the team, "Go get them." The team headed for the south side of town.

Jim Barnes, the SWAT team leader, briefed his team one last time as they headed for Delaware Street. "Okay, we have four known doors leading outside from this structure. We have the front door and the back door to the house itself, and the garage door and an additional door leading into the back yard from the garage. You know your assignments. You four, including you guys from the local office, will cover the garage entrance and back door exit, while the rest of us hit the front and back doors of the house simultaneously. When we breach the doors, we will be using stun grenades, do don't be alarmed at the explosions. Don't leave your posts until you hear one of us yell, 'CLEAR!' at the garage door and the back garage door. If someone tries to make a break through either garage door, use whatever force is necessary to stop them - but try not to shoot one of my SWAT guys. If they try and escape in a vehicle, shoot out the tires before you start shooting into the vehicle. Any questions? Good." He called the guys in the apartment across the street from the house, and got the word that nothing had changed at the Delaware Street address.

The two guys that would be guarding the back door to the garage, and the four guys that would be going into the house from the back door of the house itself, were let out of the SWAT van on Maryland Street, one block west from Delaware. They had to climb over a four-foot chain link fence, but there were enough tall weeds and garbage in the back yard of the house to hide their approach, unless someone was actually on the lookout from the back windows of the one-story house on Delaware.

The van drove around the block to Delaware, and the remaining team members piled out and took their positions. If they had been lucky enough to get more time, they would have run cameras up to the house windows to see who was in what room in the house. Unfortunately, because they were worried that someone would tell the terrorists about the team watching the house from across the street, they had to move fast and would be going in blind.

The "door breacher" two-man teams had two jobs. First, one of the guys had to place a small explosive charge around the door handle and lock of the door. This was done (by two different breachers) to both the front and back doors. Once the explosive charge was detonated, the second breacher had to swing a heavy post up against the door, hopefully forcing the door open. All of this was supposed to happen within about three seconds. Once the doors were forced open, other team members would toss in stun grenades. The team was prepared with ear and eye protection devices, so that the grenades would not keep them from being able to move after the grenades exploded. The idea was that the people in the house would be incapacitated by the grenades, making it easy for the SWAT team to move in and capture the house occupants without violence. In a bigger house, bedroom windows would have been broken and stun grenades used in those rooms, too - but this house was small enough that the team felt that grenades in the front and back of the house would suffice to cover every room in the house, except for the garage - and that is one reason the team had people watching the garage entrances.

Barnes waited until he heard from the back-door breach team before turning everyone loose.

"Front door wired and ready."

"Back door wired and ready."

The team leader started the fireworks. "Both teams, go on three. One, Two, THREE."

The blasts did their job. The front door hasp was torn from the lock, but was still stuck in the door jam. The second front door breacher swung his post, the door lock buckled completely, and the door swung open. The back door was not as well made, and the explosion around the lock blew that door open. So, the grenades thrown from the back of the house beat the ones thrown from the front by a couple of seconds. The teams ran into the house, with each team member assigned a sector of the first room to clear - some people looked left, some right, some across the room for people coming in through other doors. There was not anyone in the front living room when that team blasted into the house. The back-door team found two people in the kitchen unconscious from the stun grenades, and one team member quickly cuffed both of them. One of them was probably Mrs. Madison, but the team had been trained to not leave anyone behind them capable of doing harm. So, both people were cuffed as other team members moved forward, down the hall between the living room and the bedrooms. The backdoor team, even taking time to cuff the suspects found in the kitchen, were still a few seconds ahead of the front door team. But the back-door team waited on the other team, so that everyone involved had good backup coverage as they prepared to clear the bedrooms.

As the stun grenade blasts would still be affecting people's hearing, one team member used an electronic megaphone to increase the volume of what he was shouting.

"Anyone in one of these bedrooms, come out now with your hands in the air! If we have to come in after you, you may end up getting shot! Surrender now!"

One bedroom door opened, and two guys came out with their hands in the air. These were the two Afghanis, and both had sworn an oath to never be taken alive - to go down fighting if necessary. But both were somewhat stunned from the grenade strikes, cowardice won out, and both surrendered meekly. They were roughly turned to the hallway wall, frisked, and then cuffed. Others on the team cleared the bedrooms to ensure there wasn't anyone else in the house.

As the reports of "Clear!" came over the airwaves from the teams in the house, the garage backdoor team was capturing the fourth male adult in the house. Youssef had been headed out to the garage to get a broom, to help sweep the floor in the kitchen, when he heard the door blasts go off. He immediately knew the house was under assault, and dove out the back door of the garage, hoping to escape before the law enforcement team could clear the house. But when he opened the door, he found himself facing two guys with Glock pistols and laser sights aimed at his head, and he, too, simply stood there and slowly raised his hands. The house had been captured without a shot being fired.

Jim Barnes called Bill Peterson to report on what they had found. "Sir, good news and bad news. We did not get Mohammed. He was not in the house, and is still loose somewhere. No bomb, No remote. We did capture what is probably the rest of his team, and we found their pickup in the garage. It still shows signs of residual radioactivity in the bed of the pickup. We also found a laptop computer that they may have been using to communicate with whoever set this up, so maybe our IT guys can get something off that."

Bill was thrilled at what they had accomplished, while at the same time even more worried about the bomb. "Great job, Jim. Get those guys down here for questioning as soon as you can. Bring Mrs. Madison, too. We'll probably charge her with aiding and abetting. I doubt we get anything out of these mutts, but you never know what somebody might say when you threaten

142

them with Guantanamo or solitary confinement in ADX Florence. We can also try playing one of these guys against the others, to see if anyone wants to make a deal for a lighter sentence. Also, we need that laptop as quickly as you can get it here. We'll probably send it on to the lab in D.C. after our IT guys take a quick look at it. That may turn out to be the key to locating the bomb, and we need all the help we can get. Thanks again for the fast action on this. I know you prefer more prep time, but your guys did good, considering what they were up against. It could have easily gone the other way."

Jim Barnes promised to get everyone down to the Federal Building as quickly as possible. Bill hung up, and wrote a quick email to the Director and Randy Marshall to bring them up to date. Bill then called Glenn Simpson, to thank him again for the intel assist and tell him about the successful raid.

"Glenn, we got most of them, and hopefully enough intel to help us find the bomb. I'll keep you updated, but it looks a little more likely that you might get to keep eating lunch at the Union League."

Glenn laughed, but then got serious. "We haven't won the game yet - just leading in the late innings. We still have to recover that bomb before I'll feel it is over."

Chapter 16

Things were looking up a bit in Dallas, too. The search warrant for the shrimp boat in Louisiana had included all personal property on the boat, and so the captain's cell phone was available for review. The outgoing call register showed a call going to a Dallas Area Code cell phone number on the Sunday evening the fish box transfer took place. After questioning, the boat's captain admitted that he had been given instructions to call that number when approaching port. While professional spies would have used a "burner" phone, getting rid of that phone after it was used, the Dallas right wing people were not that experienced. The cell phone was triangulated and tracked to a motel in South Oak Cliff, in the southern part of Dallas.

One agent went into the motel office and asked for a room. "I'd like the one on the far end, at the end of the curve."

The desk clerk shook his head. "You don't want that one - you get a lot of traffic noise that close to the highway. We usually make that one our last room to rent."

The agent just handed over his credit card. "Nope. I'm a retired trucker, and the road noise helps me to sleep. That's why I always ask for the room with the most noise."

The desk clerk thought to himself, "Well, it takes all kinds..." and handed the guy a keycard for the room on the far end. From that room you could see the doors of every other room along the strip motel. Two guys went into the motel room, and they soon had an observation post established at the room's only window. The motel rooms opened directly out onto the parking area, so it was fairly easy for the team to watch the comings and goings of people renting rooms. Within a few hours they had identified the rooms of the group having the cell phone in question. There were three guys staying in two adjoining rooms near the center of the motel strip.

A SWAT team was assembled and in place by late that evening. The only difference in the attack technique in Dallas was that the SWAT team obtained pass keys to allow entry into the two rooms in question from the motel desk clerk. One agent stayed with the desk clerk while the other agent went to hand out the keys. The one staying with the desk clerk was there to make sure the clerk did not phone the guys in question and warn them of the impending assault.

The pass keys were used, flash-bang grenades were tossed into both rooms, and then the teams rushed in. All three suspects were incapacitated from the stun grenades, so there was no resistance. The rooms held a lot of firearms, but, again, no bomb and no remote detonator.

The three guys were identified, and one matched the description of one of the guys that had helped to pick up the fish box in Louisiana. But once more the assault had missed the team leader. Brady Worthington was still on the loose, and it was assumed that he had the bomb, the remote, or both with him. An all-points bulletin went out across the area for Worthington. It noted that he was to be considered armed and dangerous.

Chapter 17

Thursday, May 28th

No one was talking. The alleged terrorists in Chicago had quickly lawyered up and refused to say a word. The two from Afghanistan had been identified in a photo lineup by John Bradley, the Grant, Michigan Chief of Police, as the two he had been following when he was shot. No charges had been filed, but the press was all over the arrests, wanting to know if the assault had any connection to the atomic bomb supposedly located in the Chicago area. Bill Peterson now had one of the FBI's public relations people from Washington assigned full time to his office in Chicago, just to handle all the press requests. Bill was not granting any interviews at all, claiming press of business.

In Dallas, the arrest of the three guys in the motel had not attracted that much attention - most of the crime reporters in the area, both from the local television stations and the area newspapers, skipped over that arrest report as just another drug bust of some sort. Since charges had yet to be filed in that case, those arrests were not newsworthy in the eyes of the reporters. That would change when they actually went to court and charges were revealed, but the FBI hoped to keep that from happening until at least after the weekend. That would give them more time to look for Worthington, without hopefully pushing him into fleeing the area completely.

When Bill Peterson walked into his outer office that Thursday morning he had three people already waiting to see him. One was an agent he recognized as being on his IT staff, but he couldn't remember the agent's name. The other two were Melissa Anderson and Andy Renner, the agent they had assigned to check out the boats in Port Hope, Michigan. Bill nodded at all of them. "All of you grab a cup of coffee and come on in. If you are waiting this early in the morning, I expect it is good news." That got a laugh out of Bill's admin assistant, Cindy Wade. The others smiled, got a cup of coffee from the coffee maker in the corner, and followed Bill into his office.

"Okay, one at a time, but what do you have for me?"

The agents looked at each other, and then the agent from IT stood up and spoke first. "Sir, I'm Roger Handsby from IT. We met when you first came aboard and made your tour around the office."

Bill was glad that Roger had offered his name. He didn't want to have to admit to having forgotten it. He remembered thinking when he was first introduced to Roger that he looked like the stereotypical IT guy. Glasses, pens in his shirt pocket, tie askew. "Glad to have you here, Roger. What have you got?" Bill knew that IT people tended to want to provide all the background information before they got to their point, so he was hoping he could push Roger toward revealing whatever had brought him to Bill's office.

Roger beamed. "Well, we copied that laptop computer's hard drive before we shipped it off to our lab in Washington. We knew that you wanted whatever information we could get off that computer as soon as possible, and we thought we could be looking while it was in transit to D.C. The laptop was encrypted, but they used a commercial encryption system that has a working agreement with the Agency. They have given us a backdoor into that system that allows us to break the encryption when necessary for national security. We obtained a quick court order last night that gave us permission to break their encryption, so we can now read everything on their computer.

There was not much there. A couple of innocuous games, but no information as to where they might have stashed the bomb, where Mohammed might be holed up, or much of anything of value at all - except for one thing. They had an email account on the computer, and using a recovery program we were able to reestablish a couple of the messages they had created. Both were set up as draft messages, and then erased by someone else using this same email account from somewhere else. The messages themselves were obviously coded, as both just appeared to be simple phrases. But what was really interesting was that the original email account had been established at a URL in North Korea. So, whoever these guys were talking to probably have some connection with the powers that be over there. Obviously, these guys are not Korean, so we don't know how that email location ties into these guys or the bomb - but we thought it was important enough to bring it to your attention."

Everyone else in the room was stunned. Bill finally said, "Thanks, Roger. Good work. We didn't have any idea that the North Koreans were involved in this caper. You have opened an entirely new line of inquiry for the Bureau to pursue, and we'll probably have to get other agencies involved in this, too. Let us know if you find anything else useful on that hard drive, and get with your counterparts in D.C. to let them know what you have found. I need to go to the Director with this information, so as soon as you have confirmation from Washington let us know. Obviously, and this applies to all of you, this needs to be held in total confidence. Roger, you are welcome to stay and hear the rest of this, or you can head back to your lab - your call." Roger quickly sat back down. "Okay, Melissa, what do you two have for me?"

Melissa looked over at Andy. "This is his information. I'm just tagging along. Andy, tell us what you found in Port Hope."

Andy stood up, but Bill motioned for him to sit back down. "We aren't that formal here. You don't have to stand up just to make a report." Bill realized that he should have said the same thing to Roger, but there wasn't anything Bill could do about that now.

Andy sat down, and looked down at his notes. "The Michigan Secretary of State's office was very accommodating when we asked for information on clear titles. They have everything computerized, and were able to filter their information by location to give us exactly what we needed. We found two boats completely paid for in all of Port Hope. One is about thirty years old, and the boat's captain made payments to the bank for years until that boat was paid for.

The other boat is more interesting. It was purchased in Florida three years ago, from a dealer in the Miami area, and then the new captain and a mate cruised the ship all the way up the Eastern Seaboard, and then back down the St. Lawrence Seaway to Lake Huron. When the boat was registered with the Michigan Secretary of State's office the title was free and clear. The captain, Pete Hanson, had an older boat that he sold when he bought this new one. That one also had a clear title when he sold it. We haven't been able to access the captain's bank account records at this point, and don't want to do so because it is a small town, and he would probably get wind of that search. So, we don't know how much the captain had in his account when he bought the boat. A 35-foot Bertram Sports Fisherman starts at about $650,000. We did make inquiries through our Miami office about the boat dealer, and they tell us that dealer is a little shady, and has been known to sell boats for cash without reporting that fact. A lot of drug dealers apparently want to do business that way, so this boat dealer is accommodating.

So, we may have found our guy. We don't have enough evidence yet to ask for a search warrant, so we can't officially check the boat for residual radioactivity. However, when the boat is out fishing, we can use a Geiger counter on the dock area at his boat slip, to see if we get any hits there. I'm here today to ask for permission to see what we get at the boat slip. We can have a couple of guys pretend to be looking for a fishing spot, with the Geiger counter hidden in one of their tackle boxes. We should be able to get away with that without anyone noticing anything out of the ordinary, and that might confirm where the bomb came into the U.S. Your thoughts?

Bill thought for a moment. "Okay, set it up. But make sure you search the entire dock, and not just Hanson's boat slip. We have enough information to show a good reason for searching that dock, but we need readings from every slip. We may even need to search a few additional marinas just to show we were being thorough. That way Hanson's lawyer can't come at us with an illegal search complaint after we arrest this guy. Make sure his boat is gone for the day before you do the search. Good work finding this guy - I wasn't sure this idea was going to work, so I need to call Randy Marshall in Dallas and let him know his idea paid off in spades.

Melissa, start thinking about what we would need to do to put a loose tail on this guy if he turns out to be whom we think he is. We would probably need to get the Coast Guard involved, to provide us with radar coverage to see if he is meeting other boats. See if there is someplace we can set up an over watch where we can see his boat slip. And once we get the Geiger counter results, we will probably have enough information to pull his phone records. We can probably do that without setting off any alarms. I agree with you that it would be difficult to get his bank records without him finding out that we are looking at him, and I don't want him to get paranoid until we have the stuff we need to nail him. Again, good work, all of you. We're getting close to finding the bomb and our perps - I can feel it. And all of you are helping to make that happen. You can be proud of the work you are doing. Now get back to it!"

Chapter 18

Bill had two visits to make, and he wasn't sure how they were going to go. His plan was to grab a quick lunch, and then go see the alleged terrorists being held at the Metropolitan Correctional Center, the place where all federal prisoners are held prior to and during their court proceedings. He knew that the chance of getting something out of them was slim, but he wanted to try.

He then planned to visit Chet Kingsley, his old number two, who was now in one of Chicago's Gateway Foundation Alcohol and Drug Treatment Centers, on Kedzie Avenue. Chet had been in their rehabilitation program for over a week, and was now allowed to have visitors. Bill wanted to check on Chet's progress, and to provide the guy what support Bill could give. Chet wasn't about to get out - it was a thirty-day program - but Bill had promised to check in on Chet, and Bill was going to live up to his promise.

But when he tried to back his car out of his designated parking space in the basement parking garage of the Federal Building, he was waylaid by a young blond lady holding a microphone, being tailed by a guy with a camera. Bill's first thought was that they needed to improve security in that parking garage, but then he smiled and rolled down his car window.

"Yes? May I help you?"

"Agent Peterson?" Bill didn't even try to correct the lady as to his title. "Annie Jones from ABC7 Chicago. Would you care to tell us about the people you arrested in the house on Delaware Street? Are they the ones that have the atomic bomb? Did you find the bomb?"

Bill smiled at the camera. He put his car in Park, reached across to the front passenger seat for his briefcase, opened it, and pulled out a copy of the press release prepared by FBI Headquarters. He handed that to the reporter, who looked down at it, confused.

"Off the record?" He said.

The lady smiled, showing a mouthful of perfect teeth. "Sure!" She was nodding excitedly, about to get a scoop.

Bill smiled again. "No comment." He rolled up the car window, and backed out of the parking space, nearly hitting the cameraman. As he drove off, he could see the reporter with a rather dejected look on her face, and he wondered if he had made an unnecessary enemy. He knew that fighting with the press was a no-win battle, but he was under orders not to say anything at this point, and he was determined to follow those orders if possible. He wanted to laugh at the look on her face, but thought that she might see him laughing, and that might make her even madder. He thought to himself, "Maybe I can make it up to her at some point in the future, if I can find a way to do that without compromising a case or my ethical responsibilities." He then shook his head, knowing that such a chance would probably never come.

Thirty minutes later he was at the Metropolitan Correctional Center, also known as MCC Chicago. He parked, went inside, and showed his credentials. He was told that the alleged terrorists were still meeting with their new lawyers, so that he would have to wait a few minutes before he could question them. He told the MCC guards that he didn't want to question the prisoners, but just to talk to them and their lawyers for a couple of minutes. The guards said they would speak with the attorneys and see if they were amenable to his request. A few minutes later the chief guard came back into the waiting room and told Bill that the prisoners and their attorneys would give him five minutes. Bill had to surrender his firearm before he could enter the meeting room, but that was standard procedure and he was used to the requirement.

He walked into a room where all four suspects were sitting with their attorneys. He knew this by itself was unusual, as in most cases suspects were kept separate from each other, and only allowed to visit with their lawyers until they were arraigned. But he had asked to have everyone together in a single room. He was also surprised that there wasn't a translator present, which told him that all the suspects spoke excellent English.

"Good afternoon. For those of you that don't know me, I'm Special Agent in Charge Bill Peterson, head of the Chicago FBI office. I'm sure you have all been told by your attorneys not to answer any questions, so I'm not going to ask any. I just want to let you know what is probably going to happen to each one of you. After your meeting with your attorney ends, by law we cannot ask you any additional questions, so you will be released into the General Population cells of this prison. Probably different cells for each of you. The word will soon get out amongst the prisoners in those cells that you are the ones being held as possible terrorist suspects. I don't know how those rumors spread - it may be the guards, or some prisoner may have overheard something as you went through the check-in procedure here at the prison.

At that point, as the word gets out about your alleged crimes, your life expectancy will drop to nearly zero. The GenPop cells in MCC are, unfortunately, pretty much run by the Chicago gang groups that we arrest frequently on drug, robbery, and murder charges. I wish the guards here had a better handle on things, but that internal social structure is pretty typical of any prison in the United States, other than the SuperMax site in Colorado. While our gangbangers don't represent the best citizenry of the Chicago area, one thing they are, almost to a man, is extremely patriotic. When they find that they have some potential terrorists in their midst, you may not be long for this world. Rape is a good possibility, and then you may end up with a homemade shiv in your back. I'm aware of what the Prophet said about a martyr's death - but I'm not sure that getting murdered in prison qualifies you for that title.

However, if you tell your attorney that you are willing to make a deal with the authorities, and reveal what you know about where we can find Mohammed and the bomb, then you will NOT be placed in General Population, and you have a much better chance of making it to trial. At the trial, your cooperation will be made known to the judge. I'm not promising anything, but that cooperation could result in a lighter sentence for the person or persons that give us vital information.

So, once this meeting is over, you will be separated, and, with your attorney present, asked if you would like to volunteer any information. If not, you will be treated just like the ordinary prisoner you are. That is not a threat, but just a statement of fact about the way things are. Your attorneys may advise you against making any such a deal, but remember, they are not the ones going into the general population cells - you are. If you don't make it until Monday, alive that is, it is no skin off their backs - they get paid either way, and they will quickly get another case assigned Monday morning. Again, this is not a threat - I'm just telling you the way it is. Hope to see all of you at the arraignment on Monday. Thanks for your time, and you may now continue your meeting." Bill turned around and walked out without waiting for comments or questions. The attorneys were of course all sputtering, but Bill didn't care.

He told the agents waiting outside the meeting room what he had suggested to the group, and they all smiled. One agent said, "Want to take a bet on how many want to make a deal?" Bill just shook his head. "Nope. But all we need is one."

Bill went back to the reception area, collected his gun, and left the facility.

He thought about Chet and his rehab stint. Bill didn't know what to expect at the rehabilitation facility. Some people do well in rehabilitation, but he knew there was a high percentage of recidivism after release from rehab. To become an FBI agent takes a pretty strong-willed person, someone with a lot of built-in self-discipline. Bill knew that Chet had that level of self-discipline, but what Bill didn't know is whether or not Chet could apply that to help overcome his addiction.

Bill pulled into the Gateway facility parking lot, locked his car, and headed inside. Here he found a small reception area, with a gentleman behind a window with a sliding glass door, similar to what you see in a doctor's waiting room. The guy behind the window slid it open.

"Yes, may I help you?"

"Hi. I'm Bill Peterson. I'm here to see Chet Kingsley. I called this morning."

The guy behind the desk consulted a clipboard. "Yes, here you are. I do have a question for you, before you go in. Our notes state that you are an FBI agent, and Mr. Kingsley's boss. Is that correct?"

"Yes."

"Are you armed?"

"Yes, why?"

"We ask that all firearms be locked up out here in our reception area. Unfortunately, some of the patients we get are close to suicide when they arrive, and we don't want to tempt anyone with the possibility of grabbing a loaded weapon."

"Makes sense." Bill took out his pistol, and ejected the magazine. "What is your procedure for locking up a firearm? I need to make sure I can get it back when I leave."

The guy behind the counter pointed at what looked like a group of mailboxes in one corner of the reception area. "You lock up your gun in one of those boxes, and you keep the key. We do have duplicate keys, just in case, but please try to not lose your key!"

Bill smiled, and locked his pistol in the storage box.

A door buzzer sounded, and a door opened at one end of the reception area. Bill walked through, and looked around. The place reminded him of something, and then he finally realized what that was. The place looked like an Embassy Suites Hotel, if the hotel was cut down to five stories. A big courtyard, pathways leading to various small meeting areas around the courtyard, and a soaring atrium with elevators in the corners. A couple of the meeting areas held groups involved in what Bill assumed were some sort of therapeutic discussions, and one guy got up from the nearest group when he saw Bill. The guy was wearing a nametag that said, "Dr. Bill."

"Hi! You must be Bill. I'm Bill, too, Doctor Bill Champagne. But everyone around here just calls me Dr. Bill." They shook hands.

"I guess you know I'm here to see Chet Kingsley. What can you tell me about how he is doing?"

"Not much I can say about his treatment or official prognosis, without violating HIPPA laws. However, since you are his boss, and the one that recommended treatment, I can tell you, off the record, that he is doing great. I would say he has a great chance at a full recovery, if you understand that once an addict, always an addict, and you must always be on guard against relapses. Come on, I'll take you to him. He's out back, sitting in the shade and reading."

They wandered through the indoor pathways, over the fake streams and waterfalls, and reached a back wall sliding door.

"Chet is in a sitting area just to the right, just past the door. We ask that you hold your visitation to no more than thirty minutes. And if you don't mind, I want to get back to my group discussion. When you're ready to leave, just walk back up to the door where you came in. We have cameras monitoring everything, and the receptionist will see you at the door and let you back out into the reception area. Thanks for coming to see Chet. Everyone we have in here needs an outside support group, and not everyone gets that support. I'm sure he will appreciate seeing you, even under these circumstances." They shook hands again, and Dr. Bill headed back to his group. Bill Peterson opened the sliding door, and stepped out into what looked like a fancy garden at some wealthy plantation owner's place in the south - except this was completely enclosed by a huge domed ceiling, making it usable year-round. And, Bill thought to himself, making it difficult for someone to escape over the walls. He looked to his right, and there was Chet.

Chet put down his book and stood up as Bill approached. Chet smiled, but looked a bit uncomfortable. Bill shook his hand, and motioned for Chet to sit back down.

Bill looked Chet right in the eyes, which were clear. "You look like shit."

Chet laughed. "Well, you try beating a monkey like the one I had on my back. For three days they just about had to tie me to my bed, because otherwise I was climbing the walls. I finally got the shit out of my system, and the cravings have lessened in intensity - but to be honest with you, they are still there. I don't know if they will ever go away completely. And now that you mention it, you don't look so good yourself. Obviously, you haven't found your bomb, or you wouldn't be coming here, hat in hand, begging for my help."

Bill laughed with him. "Actually, the doc says you are doing great. I know it will be a while before you are ready to get out of here and get back to work, but I think we can find a way to get you back as an agent. I talked to headquarters, and they seem willing to give you a second chance."

Chet slumped with relief. "You don't know how much better that makes me feel. I'm a workaholic, and that job was my life. I don't know what I would do if I had to find something else. I don't think I could survive as Mr. Mom. The kids would drive me crazier than I already am. So, tell me what you've done to find this bomb. I know you are Mr. 'Think Outside the Box,' so maybe I need to be the one to help you get back to good old regular detective work, so that we can solve this one."

Bill told Chet about the possible second bomb in Dallas, and how both offices thought the conventions were being targeted. Bill talked about the assault on the house on Delaware Street, and told Chet about what Bill had said to the suspects earlier that afternoon. They talked about how they had identified the boat used to smuggle in the bomb, and how they might could use that information to either help build a case, or as a possible trap for a future smuggling operation. Bill talked about how frustrated he was at trying to find Mohammed. Before they knew it, their thirty minutes were up, and Bill knew he had to leave. They stood up, and shook hands again.

Bill said, "I'll come back next week, if at all possible. Unless the bomb goes off, and in that case visitors will be the least of your worries."

Chet laughed. "I'll hold you to another visit. I really enjoyed getting to talk shop a little. This twelve-step stuff is good for me, but I do miss going after the bad guys. I can't wait to get back!"

Bill nodded, turned, and walked back to the front of the facility. He knew that Chet would be watching, but Bill didn't look back.

He got buzzed back into the reception area, recovered his pistol, and got back in his car. He knew he should go back by the office, but it was 4:30 on a Friday afternoon, and he had not spent much time with Julie all week. He used the voice dial blue tooth speaker built into his car, and called his wife.

"Hi, sweetheart! What's for dinner?"

"Does that mean you might actually be home at a reasonable hour tonight, so that we can share a meal together?"

"On my way now. It will probably take me an hour in traffic, but I should be there around 5:30. Do you want to eat at home, or go out somewhere?"

"I had a feeling that you might get off early tonight, so I've had a roast cooking in the crockpot all day. I should have dinner on the table when you get home, unless you want to unwind with a cocktail or two before we eat. What's your preference?"

"Dinner, then a drink, then bed. I just want some time with my beautiful Texas wife, a lady I don't get to see often enough these days."

"Flattery might get you somewhere if you're not careful. Okay, dinner at 5:30. Love you."

"Love you, too. See you in a bit!"

He got a call from Andy Renner as Bill was stuck in traffic, on the way home.

"Hi, Boss, Andy Renner at the office."

"What did you find on our Mr. Hanson?"

"We got a hit on our Geiger counter on the pier in front of Pete Hanson's boat dock. I think we have enough to go for a search warrant."

"Let's hold off on the search warrant. In fact, we probably just need to turn this one over to the Detroit office. They can watch this guy much easier than we can from here in Chicago."

Andy sounded disappointed. "Okay, boss, your call."

Bill tried to cheer up his employee. "Andy, we don't need to search the boat. What we want to do is catch this guy bringing in another terrorist, or another bomb. I don't see how we could establish an observation post in a place like that, so the best we can do is send in one of our fake utility trucks and set up some cameras on poles looking down at the docks. Agents can watch to see how many people Hanson takes out on his fishing trips, and how many he brings back. But we need to be prepared to move if he brings in someone illegally, and that is where I think the Detroit office comes in. If you want to be the one to set up the surveillance, be my guest. We could then turn it over to the Detroit office for them to babysit. I'm worried that we're getting too strung out, trying to handle this case across several states, and we need to be concentrating on finding our bomb. You agree?"

"Sounds good, boss. I'll get started on setting up the surveillance. My team knows the site, and they can make recommendations on where to place cameras."

"Thanks, Andy. And if we do end up catching another bad guy that Hanson is trying to smuggle in, I'll make sure that you

get the credit you deserve for helping to
break that part of the case."

Chapter 19

Dinner was a smash hit. As per their habit, they spent dinner talking about Julie's day. She told Bill about the things she had bought for the condo, how she planned to rearrange the furniture, and about the two little old lady neighbors she had met that lived across the hallway. They had kept peeking out their door every time she had come and gone from the apartment until she finally had enough, knocked on their door, and introduced herself.

"They seemed impressed that there would be an FBI agent living in the building. Either that, or they were worried they would get busted when we smelled the pot wafting out from under their door."

Bill smiled. "These days, almost anyone can get a prescription for medical marijuana. I'm not going to give them a second look, unless they are rolling doobies on the front steps of our building."

They cleaned up the remaining dinner dishes. Julie had cleaned some of the pots while she was waiting for Bill to get home, so it didn't take that long. They poured a couple of cocktails, and moved back into their living room. "Okay," Julie said. "Tell me about your day."

Bill told her about finding the smuggler, but left out the news about the North Koreans. Some information was too sensitive to be shared, even with your wife. He told her about his run in with the television reporter, and what he had told the suspects when they had gotten to the Metropolitan Correctional Center. By this time, she was laughing so hard she nearly spilled her remaining drink.

He got more serious when he told her about his visit to Chet Kingsley. "He is improving, but still looks pretty bad. We did have a good time talking about our cases. I think he misses that a lot. I hope he makes it through rehab. I could sure use him back at the office. He did say one thing, and I've heard this before from others. He called me, 'Mr. Think Outside the Box.' I don't know if that is a good thing, or a bad thing. Sometimes it is good to look at cases different ways, but some things need to be done by the book. I don't want to be known as someone that is always on a different wavelength."

Julie shook her head. "You guys seem to be obsessed with boxes. Either you are thinking in or outside the box, checking off boxes, trying to box in a suspect with your interview technique, or wrapping a case up in a box with a ribbon. I'm surprised you don't have a boxing ring in that basement gym at the Federal Building."

Bill smiled. "Actually, there is a ring, but most agents prefer to practice hand to hand combat instead of boxing. But it is still known as the boxing ring."

Julie crowed, "See? I told you so!" Bill kissed her.

They tossed down the rest of their drinks. Hand in hand, they strolled back toward their bedroom.

Chapter 20

Friday, May 29th

Bill woke early, with something tugging at his subconscious. He had a nagging feeling that he had missed something from his conversations on Thursday, but he couldn't figure out what had skipped past him without registering. He quietly slipped on a pair of gym shorts and some running shoes, and headed out the door. Usually a run helped him to clear his mind.

He did three miles in about twenty minutes, and was happy with his time. There was a day when he could have done it in eighteen, but he figured that at his age twenty wasn't bad at all. He jogged through a pretty quiet Chicago, with only a few delivery trucks on the road that early. But the nagging thought in the back of his mind still wouldn't crystalize. He shook his head in frustration when he got back to the door to their condo.

Julie was up, and cooking breakfast. He gave her a quick kiss on the back of the neck, but when she complained about the way he smelled, he headed for the shower.

"Make it a quick one. Breakfast will be ready in about five minutes."

"Okay, a quick shower. Want to join me?" Julie just shook her head.

Bill turned on the shower head, and quickly stripped off his running gear. The hot water felt good against his back, after his run. He was rubbing shampoo into his hair when it finally hit him. Hot water. From a hot water heater. And there had been a hot water heater cardboard box in the garage at the house in Grant where the sheriff had gotten himself shot. He thought, "Could it really be just that easy?" He quickly rinsed and shaved, and started getting dressed. He heard Julie call, "Breakfast," and he headed for the kitchen.

"Sweetheart, you're not going to believe this, but your rant about boxes last night has given me another avenue to check out on our case. If you helped to solve this one, I'll buy you dinner anywhere in town you want to go." Julie just smiled. "I'll hold you to that, but now you need to put on your tie and go do big things."

Bill grabbed tie, quickly tying a four-in-hand knot he had learned from his dad, and picked up his coat and briefcase. He gave Julie a long kiss, and promised to call her later if he had any news. He headed downtown, feeling better than he had in weeks.

For once there wasn't anyone waiting for him when he got to the office. He jumped on his computer, ignored the emails that had piled up in his absence on Thursday afternoon, and called up the report from the Michigan State Police CSI team on the house in Grant. There it was, about the eighth item listed. "One cardboard box, for a Rheem Triton Industrial Water Heater." Bill wondered how they had all missed that possible clue. A lake house, even one rented out on a regular basis, would not have a need for an industrial sized water heater. So, what was that box doing in that garage?

He pressed his intercom button. "Cindy, please see if you can get me the manager of the McCormick Center on the phone."

"Yes, Sir."

Three minutes later his phone buzzed. "John Smolinsky from the McCormick Center on line one."

Bill pushed the button for that line on his phone. "John, this is Bill Peterson from the Chicago FBI office. I have a plumbing question about the McCormick Center, and probably need to talk to one of your plumbers. Is it possible to get somebody on the phone that can talk plumbing 101 to somebody that knows nothing about plumbing?"

John said, "Give me a couple of minutes, and I'll get somebody to call you back. Give me your number. This have something to do with the convention?"

Bill said, "Just a long shot at this point, and I'm basically just looking for information. Thanks for your help."

Bill gave John the phone number for the direct line to his office, and they hung up.

Five minutes later Bill got another call.

"Hi! This is Woody Calhoun. I'm a plumber here at McCormick. Mr. Smolinsky said you had some questions about our plumbing?"

"Thanks for calling back so quickly. My question is simple. Do you use industrial sized water heaters at McCormick?"

"Nope." That answer had Bill deflating like a balloon. He thought he had solved this case, but it looked like this was just another dead end. But the plumber continued. "We just use regular sized heaters. That's all we need in our restrooms. We've thought about putting in an industrial heater for the dishwashers in our kitchen, but we have three regular heaters set up in sequence for that operation, and that seems to be meeting our needs. Why are you asking about industrial heaters? Those are mostly used in hotels and big restaurants."

Bill sat back up. "So, hotels and restaurants need the extra hot water capacity?"

"Yep. Almost every hotel where I've done work uses some sequence of industrial heaters for hot water for their guest rooms. And some have extras for pools, hot tubs, laundry rooms, and their restaurants. Industrial heaters are a big expense when building a new hotel. A plumber that gets that contract can make a bundle."

"Have you worked on water heaters at any of the downtown Chicago hotels? Do you know which hotel uses which brand of heater?"

"I know that when the Hyatt remodeled, they put in Rheem heaters. They are a little more expensive, but they last longer, and the water consistently holds the temperature where you want it. I recommend those, if that is what you are looking for."

Bill saw that as a way out of the conversation. "Thanks for the recommendation. Tell Mr. Smolinsky that I appreciate your time and advice." They hung up, and Bill wondered if he had said too much to the plumber - but he needed that information.

He was about to call the Hyatt when he got an incoming call from the Metropolitan Correctional Center. "Sir, this is Sargent Randy Pascal at MCC Chicago. It looks like whatever you said to Hamid Youssef worked. He says he is willing to talk, but will only talk to the "FBI Chief." I'm pretty sure that means you. What do you want us to do with him?"

"Is his attorney with him?"

182

"No, Sir. We asked him if he wants his attorney there, and he said no."

"Okay, put him in an interrogation room. I'll be there in about an hour. Just let him stew for that hour. And thanks for the heads-up"

"Yes, sir, no problem. Interrogation room two is open, and we'll put him in there."

Bill headed for the MCC. It was a long shot that Youssef would know where to find Mohammed or the bomb, but maybe the prisoner would have some nugget of useful information that would help the case. Bill also knew that Youssef might just be bargaining for a better deal, and not be willing to reveal anything. But it was worth the trip to try.

When he arrived at the reception area, he filled out the form required for all visitors, including law enforcement, turned in his pistol, and asked for Sargent Pascal.

The door to the interior of the prison buzzed, and a huge guy came through, ducking his head a little as he came through the doorway. "Sargent Pascal?"

"Yes, sir."

"Thanks again for calling me on this. Your size could obviously be intimidating to most prisoners. Would you be willing to stay with me, as a witness, while I interrogate the prisoner?"

The huge guard smiled. "Yes, sir. I've been used in that role before, and I know how to look menacing." The guard led Peterson to the interrogation room. The only furniture in the room was a table and two chairs. Youssef sat in one of the chairs, across the table from the door, handcuffed to cables that came up out of the floor and through the top of the table. Sargent Pascal stood just inside the door, crossed his arms, and glared at the prisoner.

Youssef actually looked relieved to see Peterson.

There was a digital recorder on the tabletop, and Peterson turned it on. "Okay, Youssef, you asked for this meeting. Attending we have Hamid Youssef, myself, FBI Special Agent Bill Peterson, and Sargent Pascal from the MCC guard force." Bill glanced at his watch. "It is 10:05 AM on Friday, May 29th. Youssef, I understand that you have waived your right to an attorney, and are willing to answer questions without your attorney being present. I want to warn you again that anything you say can and will be used against you in court. Are you still willing to waive that right to an attorney, and answer questions?

"Yes."

"Please speak up so that the recorder can hear what you have to say."

"YES."

"Okay, why are we here?"

"The Crypts are telling me that I won't make it out of the shower alive this evening - that they have big plans for me. I believe them, and I'm scared." I'm willing to tell you whatever you need to know if it will get me out of General Population."

"Okay, we need to know how to find Mohammed, and whatever information you have on the bomb."

"I don't know where Mohammed is hiding. He has a huge extended family in the Chicago area, and could be staying with any of them. If I knew, I'd tell you - but I don't have any idea."

Bill decided to take a chance. "Okay, if you can't help us, I'm leaving, and you're going back into GenPop. We know about the water heater bomb at the Hyatt, so if that is all you have, you haven't given us enough to deserve getting pulled from General Population." Bill started to get up from his chair.

"Wait! You know about the bomb at the Hyatt?"

Bill nodded, trying hard not to smile about Youssef confirming that location. "Unless you have something else to tell us...." And he again started to rise.

Youssef started squirming. "You can't send me back in there! Here's something you might not know. Mohammed had two of his cousins get jobs at the Hyatt, and they are watching the situation for Mohammed. If the bomb squad shows up, or if you start evacuating the area, they will know, and they will call Mohammed. He has promised he would go ahead and set off the bomb if that were to happen."

Bill sat back down in his chair, and thought for a moment. Well, so much for his plans to get the Chicago PD Bomb Squad to dismantle the bomb. He looked across the table at Youssef. "Anything else you have forgotten to tell me? What kind of car is Mohammed driving? I'm assuming there is a remote detonator attached to the bomb. Is there also a manual switch if the remote does not work? Where on the bomb are the controls? Give me more, or the Sargent here is going to escort you right back to the cell you came out of this morning."

Youssef put his head in his hands, which was hard to do when wearing handcuffs. "Last we saw Mohammed he was driving a red Ford Edge SUV. I don't know the model year or license plate number. It was probably registered to one of his other family members - I don't think it was in his name, like the pickup. The controls for the bomb are just under the plate separating the pump from what was the heating element on the water heater. I saw Mohammed and one of the techs from Afghanistan installing the battery for the remote in that area of the heater tank. I think that is all the controls, but I'm not sure. The rest of the bomb was in a big lead sheath, so if there are any more controls they would have to be inside that sheath."

"How did you assemble the bomb?"

"When we were at the house in Michigan, the welder used his torch to take the bottom off the water heater, the plumber pulled off all the hose connections, and we pulled all the heating elements out through that bottom opening. Then we put the water heater shell over the bomb casing. It was tight, but it did fit. We were all worried about radiation exposure, so we tried to do it as quickly as possible. The welder reattached the bottom of the heater, and we loaded the whole thing into the back of Mohammed's pickup truck. After the incident with the Sheriff, we took off for Chicago. When we moved the bomb to the Hyatt, Mohammed and the tech installed the batteries for the heater controls and for the remote detonator."

"Do you know if the bomb also has a manual detonation switch? Is there any sort of booby trap that will be set off if we disconnect the battery for the remote detonator?"

"I don't think so, but I don't know. I'm not the expert on the bomb. I do remember seeing a switch and manual timer, so I guess there is a way of setting it off manually if the remote doesn't work for some reason. I just don't know about any booby traps. I'm sorry, but I can't help you there."

Youssef just sat there, with his head in his hands. "Is that enough? Are you willing to get me out of GenPop?"

Bill thought about it for a minute. What Youssef had said did help. "Okay Sargent, put him in isolation until he is arraigned. We'll work forward from there, depending on what the judge says. And Sargent, if you say a word to ANYONE about anything you heard in here today, you'll be working in our Nome, Alaska facility by next week."

The Sargent nodded. "Yes, sir. Actually, I'm from Alaska and have been trying to get transferred back up there, but I understand the need for secrecy in this situation. I had a top-secret security clearance in the army, so I know how to keep secrets. Good luck with your bomb. I'll take care of Youssef."

Chapter 21

Bill headed back out to his car. He had a lot of things to cover, and quickly, and he almost wished he could clone himself and make about three phone calls at once. He started off calling his office. "Hi, Cindy. I'm leaving MCC and heading back in. First thing I need is the name of the manager of the Hyatt Regency down by the convention center. Find that name for me, and patch me into the hotel if you can get that person on the line. Don't tell them this is the FBI calling, I don't want to alarm them - but see if you can explain that this is important. If you can't get the manager, find out how quickly they can call me back, and give them my cell number. If possible, I would like to talk to the manager in the next fifteen minutes. Otherwise, I'm considering heading down to the hotel - it is that important. I'd rather not have to show up there, so use your charms on them."

Cindy giggled. "Yes, boss. Hang up, and I'll buzz you when I have them on the line, or I'll call you back with an update in just a couple of minutes."

"Thanks, lady. You do good work, no matter what my predecessor told me." Cindy laughed out loud at that one. Bill hung up the phone, and started driving.

Two minutes later his phone buzzed, and he used the car's blue tooth system to answer. "This is Bill."

"Hi, boss. The hotel manager is named Lisa Brooks. She was in a meeting, but her admin assistant said she would get Lisa to call you back the minute she got free, hopefully within the next ten minutes."

"Thanks again, Cindy. Okay, I guess I'll head back to the office. Hopefully this lady will call me back before I get there."

Eight minutes later Bill's phone rang. "Hello, this is Bill Peterson."

"Hi, Bill. This is Lisa Brooks from the Hyatt Regency. Your administrative assistant said this was important, so I'm calling you back."

"Thanks for getting back to me so quickly. First, are you alone in your office?"

"Yes."

"Okay. I am the Agent in Charge of Chicago's FBI office, and I have a security matter to discuss with you and your Chief Engineer, or whatever title that person uses.

Unfortunately, it can't be done over the phone. This is pretty urgent. I know it is short notice, but are you and your engineer free for lunch? Is there some place close to your office where we could meet and talk? I don't want to be seen coming into your office if possible."

Lisa was silent for a moment. "I had a lunch meeting set up, but I can postpone that until tomorrow. Would you like to come to my club for lunch? I'm a member at the Union League."

Bill laughed. "Sorry, I couldn't help it. It might be the stress is getting to me. I had lunch at the Union League earlier this week with Glenn Simpson, so this is quite a coincidence. It would be a great place to eat, so thanks for the invitation. What time would be convenient for you two to meet me there?"

"Let me get with Steve Jennings, head of our Engineering Department, and I'll call you right back."

Two minutes later Bill's phone rang again. "Steve and I will meet you there at noon. Does that give you enough time to get there?"

"I'm in my car right now. I'll go straight there. And please, don't tell anyone you are having lunch with someone from the FBI. Again, I appreciate your cooperation. I'll explain everything at lunch."

"Now you've got my curiosity aroused. This better be worth all the cloak and dagger routine."

Lisa hung up before Bill could respond.

Bill pulled into the Union League driveway thirty minutes later. He gave the keys to the valet, got his parking ticket, and walked into the reception area. He gave Lisa's name to the concierge, and a waiter guided Bill to Lisa's table. She, and the guy Bill assumed was Steve Jennings, stood up as Bill arrived.

Lisa was about Bill's age, tall, and immaculately dressed in a dark business suit. Steve was short and thin, but somehow looked like someone who could handle himself in any situation. Bill introduced himself, they shook hands, and everyone sat down. The waiter took their drink and food orders, and then left them alone.

Bill didn't waste any time. "Thank you again for agreeing to meet with me on such short notice, and away from your offices. I know you are busy people, but when you hear what I have to say I think you'll understand why we needed to do this a little differently. To start off with, Steve, I need to ask you a couple of questions, and learn a little about your background. Okay with you?"

"I guess."

"First of all, and try and be honest, how well do you operate under pressure? Can you maintain your level of coolness when things are going to hell around you?"

Steve nodded. "I spent my first two years out of college in the army, disarming IEDs in Iraq during Bush Two's little war. I think I've shown I can stay cool."

"Okay, you may just be the man I've been looking for. Next question, to both of you. What I'm about to reveal to you will be quite shocking. But I must ask that you promise to keep this a secret, just between the three of us, until things are resolved. Believe it or not, the fate of downtown Chicago might be at risk if either of you go running off at the mouth to anyone about what you are about to hear. Basically, I'm going to grant you, on my own authority, security clearances to know something that could turn out to be highly dangerous."

Lisa and Steve looked at each other, and then back at Bill. Lisa spoke first. "Okay, I'll go along with you, as long as what you are discussing is legal."

Steve added, "I'll go along with my boss. And I know about security clearances. Don't we need to sign a bunch of forms, get a background check, and all of that red tape stuff?"

Bill looked him straight in the eye. "I used the security clearance language to impress upon you how serious this situation is. There will not be any forms. I'm just going to take the word of each of you that you understand how important it is that this information does not get out to anyone."

Both Lisa and Steve nodded their assent.

They then had to wait a minute while the waiter delivered their salads and drinks. Everyone picked up a fork.

"Okay. Steve, this question may seem a little odd, considering how this conversation has been going, but bear with me. I understand, from another source, that you use Rheem Industrial Water Heaters in the hotel?"

Steve did a double take. "Yeah, we use Rheems. We have them on every floor, and several in sequence for our dishwashers, our laundry room, and even our pool and hot tub area. Why?"

"And I'm assuming you keep some spares on hand, in a storeroom somewhere, in case one of the water heaters in use breaks down?"

"Yep. We keep two fresh ones down in the basement. And we replace those as we use them. They are expensive, but they last a long time, and put out a consistent water temperature. I always thought they were worth the extra money. Is this about some sort of water heater purchase fraud?"

Bill shook his head, signaling no. "You're a little off base on this one. What if I told you that right now, in your basement, you have three spare water heaters, instead of two? And here's the kicker. One of those is not a water heater, but a half ton bomb disguised to look like a water heater."

Both Lisa and Steve dropped their forks, and just glared at Bill. This time Steve spoke up first. "You've got to be kidding."

"Nope. And here is why we're eating here, instead of meeting in your office. The terrorist that we are tracking, that planted the bomb and we think is planning on using during the Republican Convention, has managed to get at least two of his relatives hired at the hotel. They are watching our every move. If we come in with the bomb squad, or try and evacuate the hotel, they call their cousin and half of downtown Chicago gets blasted into the lake.

So, we have to find a way to dismantle the bomb without alerting the spies on your staff. Steve, your experience in Iraq may come in handy. We need a plan, and it needs to be implemented quickly and quietly, without anyone else on your staff aware of what we are trying to accomplish.

I thought a little about this on the drive over here. First, we need to set up an early warning system so that we can be alerted if someone is coming down to the basement to check on the bomb. Second, we are going to have to sneak a welder and a portable welding torch down to that storeroom, so that we can take the bomb apart, but we have to do that again without anyone being aware of what we're up to. Then we must get everyone back out of that room, again without being seen. My last question is one I don't know the answer to just yet. Do we leave the bomb down in storage, disarmed, to try and trap the terrorist when he shows up to try and set the manual timer on the bomb? Or do we go ahead and clear it out, and try and catch the terrorist some other way?

And one more thing I left out - this is not an atomic bomb, but it is what's called an RDD - a Radioactivity Dispersal Device. Once we open the bomb to try and disarm it, the bomb will start leaking radioactivity. So, we will either have to reseal the bomb, or yank it out once it is disarmed. There will be some radioactivity exposure to the people working on the bomb, the welder and the disarmament expert - and I'm hoping you will volunteer, Steve - but with the proper shielding we can hold that exposure to a minimum.

I know you have a lot of questions. Some I probably can't answer right now, like how we found out about the bomb. And I've got more for you. Steve, can you take a basement tour, and surreptitiously take a look in that storeroom, without anyone knowing you have been in there? And what access is there to that floor of the building. Elevators? Stairs? We are going to need to install cameras to give us some warning if anyone is headed that way, especially while we are trying to disarm the bomb. I need to hear first thoughts from both of you. I know you have been in brainstorming sessions before. Please treat this as such a session, and give me all your ideas as they cross your mind. I need your help. I can't handle this one by myself."

Both Steve and Lisa just sat there for a moment, stunned. Steve finally gathered his thoughts.

"I take regular walks throughout the building, so it will not be a problem to look in that basement storeroom. I'll make sure I'm alone when I check that out. As for access, there are two ways into that level of the basement. There is our freight elevator, and a stairway that winds down from behind the executive suite. That's the access that the staff uses to move in and out of the storerooms without having to share the regular guest elevators with our guests. The guest elevators don't go down to that level, so all we have are the two access points. How do you propose we get cameras in place?"

Bill thought for a moment. "We have some people that can pretend to be elevator repair people, doing regular maintenance on your freight elevator. Getting cameras in there will not be a problem. I can provide you with mini cameras for your stairway, if you can install them. They are no bigger than the tip of your finger, so they will not easily be noticed, if you can put them near a pipe or fire extinguisher or something else that will help break up the stairway walls. What we don't want is for the cameras to be on a large blank wall, because then they might contrast enough to be spotted. The cameras are simple to install - they have a sticky back, and all you have to do is press them up against the wall where you want them. They are completely wireless, so all you see is a speck on the wall. Think about where you might want to place them. I would like them at least a couple of floors above the floor where the water heaters are stored, and maybe a couple of floors below if there are additional subbasements below that level - that way we would have some warning time if someone started up or down the stairs while we were working in that storeroom to disarm the bomb. And we might need coverage on your loading dock, so that we can make sure the dock is clear when we're taking the bomb out of the hotel."

Steve shook his head again. "I still have a hard time believing there is a bomb in our hotel. But for right now I'm going to take your word for it. Someday, maybe over a beer, you're going to have to tell us how you figured this one out. And yes, I'll volunteer to help try and disarm the bomb. I would rather be the one doing it than trying to supervise someone else, especially knowing that I'm ultimately responsible, and that I could probably be doing it better than they could, anyway. So, count me in for that job. Do you have a welder in mind? I'm assuming they are going to be taking off the bottom of the water heater. The top just screws on, unless we need to get from the pump section down to where the heating elements are usually located. That may take some welding, too. I have a guy we usually hire for welding jobs. He is pretty stable, and I think he could handle this. Unless you have somebody in mind?"

Bill nodded his agreement. "Thanks for volunteering. I had a feeling you would want in on this. Get me the information on your welder, so that I can check him out. My gut feeling is that is who we will go with for this job, too. And you two now have a difficult acting job. You have to keep doing your regular jobs, just like you always do, while ignoring the fact that there is a bomb in your basement big enough to blow up several city blocks. Lisa, it looks like Steve will be busy helping us set up, and then helping us disarm the bomb. We'll probably set that up so that we're working in the middle of the night. I'm assuming there will be less traffic in the lower levels of the hotel late at night. But there is not much you can do as hotel manager, except to keep on keeping on. Can you handle that?"

Lisa just kept looking at Bill. "This is where you tell us this is all some sort of practical joke, or that we're on Candid Camera, right? I can't believe there is a bomb in our hotel. So, if you are doing this as some sort of joke, you can forget me voting to let you in here as a member. I called Glenn Simpson to check you out before we came over here, and he said that he had told you that you needed to find another member to sponsor you for membership. If this is what you are trying to pull, you can forget my vote for as long as I'm in Chicago."

Bill looked her straight in the eye. "This is not a joke. Radical terrorists have smuggled a bomb into your hotel basement, and they are looking to blow up the Republican National Convention, and half of downtown Chicago will disappear if they are successful. I could have just had lunch somewhere with Steve, but you are the hotel manager, and you deserve to know what is going down in your hotel. You have a lot to do to get ready for the convention. At your next staff meeting, can you bring up safety inspections? That will give Steve an out to get our people in to look at your elevators and install the necessary cameras. And if Steve is seen checking out the occasional fire extinguisher in the stairway to the basement, no one will bat an eye.

On the other hand, if this is too much for you to handle, even though it would be short notice, I can call the FBI Director, he will call Hyatt headquarters, and you can be transferred out of here in just a few hours. That's not a threat – but I've got to do whatever is necessary to keep this under wraps until we can get that bomb disarmed. I don't think you want that, so show me you have the fortitude to handle this situation."

"This is not a joke."

"Nope. I'm as serious as a heart attack." Can you handle this?

"I can handle this. But we need to get that bomb disarmed and out of our basement as quickly as possible. A few days of this additional stress and I may reach a breaking point. So, do what you must do, and get it done fast."

Bill nodded. "We want it done quickly, too. At least the disarming of the bomb. We need to either replace that water heater, or leave the disarmed bomb in place, until we capture the lead terrorist coming back in to try and reset the arming device. Steve, you can help us devise a plan to get the bomb out and get another water heater, or water heater shell, in its place."

The waiter brought their lunches, but Lisa and Steve weren't hungry. After a few minutes of just pushing the food around their plates, they were ready to give up. Lisa said, "Okay, we're going back to work. I'm going to get a memo out this afternoon about rechecking all our equipment – fire extinguishers, elevators, cameras and recorders, and automatic door openers. All of that falls under Steve's purview. Steve, that will give you an opportunity to get the stuff done you need done. Bill, can you get elevator repair people to the hotel this afternoon, or is that too quick? They normally wouldn't work on weekends, unless we had a breakdown, so if you can't get a crew in this afternoon we'll have to wait until Monday. What do you think?"

Bill thought about it for a moment. "Let me make a phone call on the way back to the office. Steve, what company normally does your elevator inspections?"

"We use Otis. The City of Chicago requires us to do annual inspections, and we contract with Otis to handle those, plus whatever repairs are necessary. We haven't had any major elevator malfunctions, so to date it has pretty much just been those annual checks."

Bill nodded. "Okay, our office may already have Otis uniforms on hand we can use. We've done this elevator slight-of-hand trick before in a lot of places, but I'm not sure about Chicago, so I'll have to check to see what we have. Otherwise, we'll have to borrow some shirts from the company. I'll see if we can get people to the Hyatt this afternoon. They'll also bring you the cameras we want you to install in your stairway. How many of those do you think you will need?"

Now it was Steve's turn to think. "If we can mount two cameras a couple of floors up from our equipment storeroom, and two on the floor below, coming off the loading dock, that should do it. We won't get much warning if somebody is coming up the stairs from the dock, but we could put another camera on the dock to help remedy that issue. So maybe five cameras? Plus, however many you are going to put in the freight elevator?"

"We'll bring you a half dozen, just to make sure there are no glitches. Make sure you're not seen putting them up on the stairway walls. Once the cameras are up, call me, and we'll get a monitoring station set up. Probably a repair van of some sort, parked nearby. We will want to check radio communications from the van to your storeroom, so when we come over this afternoon, we will bring you a walkie-talkie with a blue tooth earpiece to test while you are in that storeroom. We must be able talk to the people in the storeroom while they are trying to open and defuse the bomb, so that we can warn them if anyone is headed their way. Do you normally keep the storeroom door locked? Who has keys? Are they regular keys, or keycards?"

"The storeroom is normally kept locked, and there are only three people with keys, plus a set that hangs in my office for people that might need to get in there in an emergency. So, we have pretty good control on who can get in there. Of course, someone could have borrowed my office key set while

I was out of the office and made a duplicate key. My walkie-talkie works down there, so hopefully we will not have any issues with yours. If you can get your van set up quickly, I can test the walkie-talkie when I'm installing the cameras. I do want to go into the storeroom and see this alleged bomb for myself. Not that I don't believe you, but it is a big stretch. I know not to touch anything, but I am curious. My guess is that your bad guys somehow got it delivered while I was on vacation last week. And they probably had inside help to make sure the delivery was not logged. So maybe you're right about people watching the bomb, too."

Lisa asked, "So what is your timeline to get someone into that storeroom and get the bomb disarmed?"

"I'm thinking maybe tomorrow night, probably early on Sunday morning. It will probably take us a day to get the welder and his equipment ready to go, plus we want to make sure we have all our precautions in place, and that may or may not happen this afternoon. I suggest we get out of here and get to work. Steve, put your cell number in my phone, and I'll put my number in yours.

I'll try and get our "Otis crew" there around 4:00 this afternoon. We'll need to make plans for access for tomorrow night, too. Steve, maybe you could get a room at the hotel, and then sneak back down to let our people in early on Sunday morning. I don't want you in your office on Saturday night – that might raise too many suspicions. So, we need to find a way to keep you out of sight until we need you for access. My first thought is to just have you and the welder enter the storeroom, until the bomb is disarmed. Then we could bring in another crew with a water heater shell to trade out for the real bomb, and that crew could carry the bomb out through the freight elevator. Can we get access to your back dock and the freight elevator in the middle of the night?

"I can make that happen. I have gate keys, dock door keys, and the key to the storeroom. So as long as I'm there we can make this work. I like your idea of spending a few hours in one of our hotel rooms. Lisa, will you authorize room service? I could use a steak dinner..."

Lisa laughed. "I'm glad you can find a little humor is this situation. Hopefully this all works out quickly, and we can get back to normal operations. And yes, Steve, I'll authorize you a steak dinner. The condemned man deserves one last good meal."

Both Steve and Bill groaned. Lisa signed the bill for lunch, and they all headed back to their respective offices.

Chapter 22

Bill got on the phone before he even got back to his car. "Hi, Cindy. The good news is we've found our bomb. It's in the Hyatt Regency, next to the McCormick Center. First, I want a staff meeting of every department head set for 2:00. I know it is Friday afternoon, but this is important. People are going to have to cancel their golf tee times and racquetball games. Second, I need a half dozen of our super-mini cameras sent to Steve Jennings, the head of engineering at the Hyatt. Make sure we get him some that are fully charged. We're also going to need a couple of cameras set in the Hyatt's freight elevator, and we'll need a crew to install those. Next, I need a van set up for monitoring those cameras, probably one of our regular repair company vans, that will not stick out if it sits in the parking garage at McCormick or at the Hyatt. We will need that ready to go this evening, if possible. Jennings will also need one of our walkie-talkies, so that he can hear from people in the van if someone is approaching the storeroom where we will be trying to disarm the bomb. I need to know if we have Otis Elevator shirts for our guys to wear when they are installing cameras in elevators. If not, send someone to Otis and borrow a couple of shirts that will fit our electronics team guys.

Next, please get me the Director on the phone in D.C. Then you can start working on rounding up our staff, and getting the logistics started on the other stuff. Grab whatever help you need to get this done as quickly as possible. Melissa would probably be a good place to start. Do whatever you need to make this work, but get moving! I'm sorry I have to hit you with all of this on such a short notice, but things are coming to a head, and we've got to move quickly on this. So please accept my apology if I seem to be dumping on you, but I know you can handle it."

"No, problem, boss. Glad to hear about locating the bomb. I'll get right on this list of things, and I'll let you know where we stand when you get to the office. Let me connect you with the Director, if he is available."

Thirty seconds later, as Bill was just pulling out of the Union League's parking lane, his phone rang. "Mr. Director? Just a quick call to fill you in. We've located our bomb, but we still have issues on how to get it disarmed. The bomb is in a basement storeroom at the Hyatt Regency, next door to the McCormick Center. However, one of the terrorists we arrested tells me that their group has gotten a couple of people on staff at the Hyatt, and that they are watching the situation. If we send in the bomb squad, or try and evacuate the area, they will call their ringleader and he will go ahead and set off the bomb. So, we are working on a plan to get the place wired so that we can watch the watchers, and then get a team into the Hyatt in the middle of the night, probably tomorrow night, to disarm the bomb and get it out of there. We've got a lot to do to get this operation ready that quickly, but I wanted to give you a call so that you would be aware that we are making progress.

There is a good chance that the group in Dallas is using the same technique to hide their bomb – ours is disguised as an industrial water heater – so my next call is to Randy

Marshall in Dallas. He needs to be aware that their terrorists may have people watching their bomb, too.

I think we have everybody we need to make this work – it turns out that the Hyatt's chief engineer used to disarm IEDs in Iraq – plus we have our own bomb guys on staff here in Chicago. I'll keep you informed as we proceed. Any questions, before I call Randy?"

"Good job locating the bomb. You may have just saved Chicago. Let me know if you need anything to keep this operation on track. And I agree the Dallas bunch may be using the same M.O. Fill Randy in, and tell him to be careful, too. Good luck." Again, the phone disconnected before Bill could even say, "Yes, sir."

Bill pushed the button on his steering wheel that activated his phone's Blue Tooth controller. "Call Cindy." The system responded, "Calling Cindy." The phone rang, and Cindy picked it up, still talking to someone else. "Hi, boss. We're making progress. What can I do for you?"

"Please connect me with Randy Marshall in Dallas." A minute later Bill's phone rang, again. "Hi, Mr. Peterson. This is Stella Knight in Dallas, Mr. Wilson's admin assistant. He is out of the office this afternoon. Can I help you with something?"

"Stella, this is important. We have found our bomb in Chicago, and may know how your Dallas group is hiding theirs. Can you patch me through to Randy's cell phone? Is he still in Dallas, or on vacation?"

"He is still in town, just taking a Friday afternoon off. I'll connect you."

Two minutes later Bill heard Stella tell Randy that Bill was on the phone. "Okay, Mr. Peterson, I have Agent Marshall for you."

Before Bill could say anything, Randy started sputtering. "This better be damn important. I'm on the fourth tee at Brook Hollow, one of the most exclusive country clubs in Dallas, and I don't get to play here very often."

Bill interrupted him in mid rant. "Randy, we've found our bomb, and I can probably tell you within a half mile where yours is hidden. You may need to get back to your office and start investigating. Our bomb is disguised as a Rheem Industrial Water Heater, in a tube about eight feet long. Ours

215

was hidden in a basement storeroom at the Hyatt Regency, the hotel right next door to the McCormick Place Convention Center, where our convention is going to be held in a few weeks. I'll bet almost anything that your bomb is also in a hotel next to the Dallas Convention Center or stored at the convention center if they use that kind of water heater."

"The Omni would be my guess. I'll get the bomb squad right on it."

"Don't do that. We found out that our terrorists got people hired on staff at the Hyatt, and they are watching to make sure we don't try and evacuate the place or send in the bomb squad. If that happens, allegedly they will make a phone call to the guy with the remote, and he will go ahead and set off the bomb. Your guys may have the same warning system in place, so if you send in the bomb squad you may force them to set off your bomb.

We're working on a plan to get the bomb disarmed without anyone at the hotel, except the chief engineer, knowing about it. I can fill you in later, but I figured I'd better let you know what we've found, and let you start checking to see if your bomb is stored like ours is."

"Okay, you've ruined my Friday afternoon golf game, but I wasn't hitting the ball that well, anyway. I'll get back to the office and see if we can set something up to quietly check out the Omni. I'll let you know what we find."

When Bill walked into his office, Cindy intercepted him. "Your staff is waiting for you in the conference room, but the Director just called, looking for you. You might want to call him back first."

"Okay, thanks. Please see if you can get him on the phone for me."

Bill's phone was already buzzing when he got to his desk. "This is Bill."

"Did you get your info to Dallas?"

"Yes, sir, I've filled in Randy Marshall. He is going to check out similar situations around their convention center."

"Have you got a plan in place to get the bomb disarmed?"

"Yes, sir, we have the beginnings of a plan to get the bomb disarmed and out of the hotel early on Sunday morning. I'm about to meet with my team to finalize everything."

"Okay, I'm sending you a NES Team to take the bomb off your hands once you get it out of the hotel. I know it is radioactive, so we don't want it handled by anyone on the Chicago bomb squad. The team should be there later tonight. This afternoon we'll put a bomb disposal truck on a C-147 and fly that into Wright-Patterson Air Force Base in Ohio. From there they will drive that truck on to Chicago. You need to set something up to transfer the bomb from whatever transportation you use to get it away from the hotel to the NEST truck. Is there anything else you need from us in headquarters?"

"No, sir. And thanks for the help with the bomb disposal. To be honest, I hadn't gotten that far in my planning."

"No problem. I'm thinking we need to put a 'Return to Sender' sticker on the bomb and give North Korea a taste of their own medicine. Don't say anything about that idea, because I'm serious, and I'm going to take that to the President. Maybe we can get a little revenge for putting us through all of this." Again, the Director hung up before Bill could respond.

Just as Bill got ready to walk into the conference room, he got a text from Steve Jennings. "Can't believe it, but bomb is there, just like you said. I'm waiting on your cameras, and I'm going to call our welder." Bill sent him a quick text back – "Working on the cameras." He walked into the conference room, and the buzz quietened. "I guess you have all heard that we found our bomb. It's in a basement storeroom at the Hyatt Regency, next door to the McCormick Center. The kicker is that one of the terrorists we're holding at MCC tells me that Mohammed has gotten relatives hired at the Regency, and that they are watching to make sure the bomb squad doesn't show up, If that happens, allegedly they will call Mohammed and he will remotely set off the bomb. So, we need to develop a plan to handle all of this. First, we need cameras set up to watch the accesses to the storeroom, so that we can get a little warning if someone starts snooping around while we are trying to disarm the bomb. Second, we need a plan to get the bomb disarmed in place. Third, we need to get the bomb out of the hotel, and hopefully replace it with a dummy, so that the terrorists will not know we have made the switch. We want to do that to try and capture Mohammed when he shows up to see why his remote is not working during the convention. I asked Cindy and Melissa to get started setting things up for what I'm calling Operation Hyatt. Where do we stand?"

Cindy looked down at her notes. "We have eight cameras ready to go, fully charged. Two will go with the elevator repair team, and six will go to the engineer at the hotel. We did not have Otis uniforms, so I've sent Sam Donald down to their office to get a couple of shirts. We called Otis, and they are being very cooperative. Those shirts should be back here within a half hour."

Melissa chimed in. "We already had a van set up for surveillance, with signs on it identifying it as Hudson Electric. We think that will work to monitor the cameras. We need to get that into a parking lot within a couple of blocks of the hotel, or in the hotel's parking garage. We also have a twelve-passenger van that we want to use to switch out the water heaters. We've taken the seats out of that van, and we have a crew working now to build a cradle to hold the water heaters going to and from the hotel. One issue we haven't solved is the disarmament team. We don't have anyone on staff that knows how to disarm bombs, other than the basic training we all got at Quantico. What are the plans to make that happen?"

Bill nodded. "Great work. As for disarming the bomb, we're going to use the hotel's chief engineer, Steve Jennings. As it turns out, he used to disarm IEDs in Iraq during the war there. I don't think we could find a more qualified bomb disposal specialist. We're also going to need a welder, to take off the ends of the water heater so that Steve can access the bomb's controls. The engineer knows a guy he uses for welding work around the hotel, and Steve thinks this guy could handle the job. I'd rather have two guys that know and trust each other working on the bomb than to bring in outsiders, so I think this is the way I want to go, unless you folks can convince me there is a better way."

Everyone looked at each other, but no one spoke up. So, Bill continued. "Okay, who are our camera installers?" James Rollings raised his hand. "I'm one of them. Sam Donald is the other. We've done 'elevator repairs' before, so we're used to it. We'll also take your other cameras to Mr. Jennings, along with the walkie-talkie. We'll show him how to use that in blue tooth mode, so that he can speak quietly, and hear through the wireless earbud. That way we can be available if he has any questions about installing our other cameras. I do have a question. Have you found a water heater we can use as our dummy heater?"

Bill shook his head no. "No, I haven't. Melissa, call some plumbing shops, and see if anyone has a Rheem Industrial Water Heater we can use as a prop. We will have to pay for it, but I'll authorize that funding. We are going to have to take that water heater apart and take the guts out of it. All we need is the shell, and we want to make it as light weight as possible, to make it easier to get it into the hotel. That will need to be completed tomorrow, and it will give our welder some practice before he works on the actual bomb. Find us a water heater and get our welder a place to work. James, when you get to the hotel, tell Steve that we will need his welder tomorrow for our water heater, too.

Have Steve call me to confirm the guy's availability.

And while I'm thinking about it, the Director called before we started this meeting. He is sending a NES Team and a bomb disposal vehicle to take away the bomb once we get it away from the Hyatt. We need to find a place to make that transfer, away from prying eyes, once we get the disarmed bomb out of the hotel. Hopefully it will still be dark, so that will help with making the switch without anyone being aware of what we are doing. Any other questions?"

Melissa looked up. "Have you thought about radiation shielding, or monitors, for the people that will be working on the bomb? We will want as little radiation exposure as possible, but we will need monitors to find out exactly how much exposure occurs. Maybe the NES Team will have some sort of lead shielded clothing and monitors?"

Bill nodded. "Good point. Cindy, call headquarters and see what is available for shielding and monitoring. If the NES Team doesn't have anything, maybe we can borrow something from one of our hospitals. I can't see our welder working from behind a lead shielded door, so an apron, gloves, and helmet would seem to be the best bet. Let me know what you find that we can use. And Melissa, thanks for catching this. That's why we're having this meeting. I can't think of everything!" Everyone laughed and headed back to work.

Fifteen minutes later Cindy stepped into Bill's office. "The NES Team will bring extra shielding with them. How many sets do we need? How many people are you planning on being in the room with the bomb?

"Have them bring us four sets of shielding, and four monitors. It will take that many people to move the bomb once we have it disarmed, but it will still be leaking radioactivity. I liked the look of James Rollings. He looks like he works out a lot and can probably lift a ton. Have him come see me, so I can see if he will volunteer to help move the bomb. I'll be the fourth person on the team."

"Cindy shook her head. "You should be in the van, if that close. You don't need to be in that storeroom."

"I know, but I want to be there. I'm the one that figured this out, so I kind of feel like this is my baby, and I need to see it all the way through to the finish. And one more thing – we are going to need a cart to move the actual bomb, once it is disarmed. See if you can find out what plumbers use to move those heavy water heaters and get us one of those."

"Okay, boss, but I still think you're wrong to be one of the people in the storeroom."

"Cindy, Eleanor Roosevelt once said, 'It is not fair to ask of others what you are unwilling to do yourself.' I think I can add value to the team that goes into that room. And I don't want to be a leader known for staying safe while others are having to take risks. I'll be fine. But thanks for giving me an argument. I want people working for me that are willing to tell me when they think I'm wrong – which I probably will be way too often!"

Bill's cell phone rang as Cindy walked out. "Agent Peterson? This is Don Czerwinski. I'm a welder that does some work for Steve Jennings at the Hyatt, and he said you two have an interesting project for me. But he wouldn't give me any details, telling me I needed to talk to you. What do you need welded?"

"Hi, Don. If you are calling me Agent Peterson, Steve must have told you I work for the FBI. First of all, call me Bill. We don't need to be stuck on formalities. We have a very sensitive project where we are going to need a welder, but I can't talk about it over the phone. What is your schedule this afternoon and tomorrow? We need to get together as soon as possible to talk about this. We will obviously put you on the clock while we talk, so make sure you include that time when you bill us."

Don laughed. "I'm finishing up a project right now, but I should be free by around 5:30 or so. Want me to come by your office, or do you want to meet somewhere else?"

"We probably want to meet somewhere else, and not have you come here. We need to include Steve Jennings in our meeting. Do you have a favorite bar here in the downtown area where we could all get a drink and talk quietly?"

"How about Miller's Pub on Adams? That's not too far from where you are in the

Federal Building, so you could walk over. It is too far for Steve to walk, but I know he uses Uber quite a bit."

"Okay, Miller's Pub it is. I'll call Steve and make sure he can make it. Give me your phone number. If Steve has a problem with 5:30, I'll call you back. Otherwise, plan on meeting both of us there. Get us a booth if you can – I don't want to be sitting at the bar if at all possible."

Don gave Bill his cell phone number, and they disconnected. Bill called Steve Jennings. "Hey, Steve, this is Bill Peterson. Are you alone where we can talk? And did you get the cameras and walkie-talkie?"

"Yes, I'm alone, but no equipment yet."

"Okay, that stuff should be there shortly, along with our elevator crew. I just got a call from Don Czerwinski, the welder. We plan on meeting at Miller's Pub on Adams at 5:30, and I'd like for you to be there. Can you get free by then?"

"If your elevator inspection crew is done, I can make 5:30. I may not have all the cameras in place by that time, but I can come back and do that later. Is that okay?"

"I would rather you get the cameras up, so that we can check those settings this evening. I'd say to finish that up first, and then come to the bar. We'll wait for you."

"Okay, I'll be there as soon as I can. It shouldn't be much past 5:30, if at all, assuming getting those cameras in place is as easy as you say. I will have to watch for traffic in that stairway at that time of day, with people possibly finishing up their jobs and going up and down the stairs, putting stuff away before they leave for the weekend. But hopefully that won't slow me down too much. Did you tell Don what we're up against?"

"No, I didn't want to get into it over the phone. So, you get to be there when I tell him, and see if his face looks like yours did when I told you and Lisa."

Steve laughed. "Okay, see you later. Oh, one more thing. Have you thought about adding a plumber to our crew of merry men? It might be nice to have someone that knows that piece of equipment on hand, just to advise us as to what wires and parts are an actual part of the water heater, and what has been added."

"Great idea. Who do you use when you need to replace one of your water heaters?"

"We have a couple of regulars, Arnie Razolli and Benny Saracen, both of whom work for Scotty's Plumbing on South Michigan. And I know you are going to ask me which of the two I think would be better for this job. Arnie is older, and he was in the Marines, so I think he would be the guy we need."

"Okay, call him, and see if he can meet us at Miller's Pub, too. Another thought – how much room is in that storeroom? We're now talking about probably having five people in there, plus the welding equipment and a machine to suck up the exhaust from the welding. Is there enough room in there for everyone, without us all getting in the way of you guys actually doing the work?"

"The storeroom is forty by forty, and it is only about one half full. There will be room for everyone. We will have to be quiet getting the equipment we need in there, but we can do it. And once I get your walkie-talkie, I'll test it to make sure it works in that room with the door closed. Let me call Arnie. He usually takes off early on Friday afternoon, but maybe I can catch him. If I tell him it is a big project, he'll be there. I'm assuming the FBI will be paying for all of this? Both the welder and the plumber are going to be charging a weekend fee, double time for after hours work, and if they can figure out how to do it, probably a charge for working on a radioactive device. So, make sure your government credit card can handle those charges!"

"It will be worth every penny, if we can get the bomb disarmed and out of there without losing half of downtown Chicago. Thanks for the good ideas. I'll see you at 5:30, or shortly thereafter."

Bill buzzed Cindy. "We will be adding a fifth member to the team going into the storeroom, a plumber, so please make sure the NES Team has enough protective gear for everyone."

"Way ahead of you, boss. I told them to bring protective gear for ten extra people, besides whatever they needed for themselves. The team is already on their way, flying in this evening. I thought about getting them reservations at the Hyatt but decided that might be a little too much. They will be staying at the Hilton Garden Inn just up the road. So, you can thank me for saving the government several hundred bucks in hotel room rate this weekend.

The cameras and walkie-talkie are on their way to the Hyatt, along with our elevator inspection team. They should be arriving there any time now. I've called several plumbing shops and found what they use to move those big heavy water heaters – it is a four wheeled cart with a handle on one end of the cart to help with maneuverability. I've found you one for rent at a rental place just on the edge of downtown, if you need it. We're making progress!"

"Cindy, I don't know what I would do without you. Steve Jennings at the hotel suggested we add a plumber to the team. If we get the guy we want, he will probably already have one of those carts. So, we may not need to rent one of them. But after we take the bomb out of the hotel, that cart may be too radioactive to ever be used again, and it may end up getting hauled off by the NES Team and their disposal truck. We may end up having to pay the plumber for a new cart once this is done. The same may go for our van, once we use it to transport the bomb to wherever we are going to transfer it to the NES Team. I know the fire department has developed plans for hosing down potential radioactive material. I don't want to contact them now, but once we get the bomb disarmed and gone, we may want them to try and clean out our van with some of their high-pressure hoses. Add that to your list, but that is something we don't have to worry with right now.

Okay, I'm leaving the office. If anyone wants to know where I am, tell them I went out for a drink. I actually am going to a bar, Miller's Pub, but it is to meet with Steve Jennings, our welder, and our plumber. I need to fill everybody in on what we are doing, and our plan. And after I tell them, I have a feeling they may all want a drink! Thanks again for all your help. Call me if you need me."

Bill grabbed his coat and headed for the elevator. He thought that he could probably use a drink, too, but he knew that under the circumstances he would have to wait until this was over, one way or the other. He called Julie while he was walking. "Hi, sweetheart! Just calling to fill you in. I'm on the street, so I can't say much. We've made a lot of progress since I left this morning, and things will be coming to a head this weekend. What would you think about getting out of town for the weekend? It might be better if you flew down to Waco to see your Mom. Yes, I will be fine here, but I just thought we might get you out of town, just as a precaution. I don't think anything will happen, but I couldn't bear the thought of anything happening to you. Would you be willing to go?"

Julie was quiet for a moment. "My first thought is that my place is here, by my husband. But there is a chance, even though it is a slim one, that after last night I may be expecting. I was going to wait until I was sure to tell you, but this changes things. So maybe it would be better if I left town. When can I come back?"

"This will all be over, one way or another, by Sunday morning. So, you can spend a long weekend with your Mom, and come home anytime after that. I'll miss you, but I think this is probably for the best. Thank you for being so understanding. You being out of harm's way will help me to concentrate on what we need to do here, because I'll know you're safe. I love you."

"Love you, too. When can I expect you this evening?"

"Don't know when I'll be home. Right now, I'm going out drinking."

"Say, what?"

"Just kidding, sort of. I'm meeting some of the guys that we need to hire to help us get this done, and we're meeting at Miller's Pub down here close to where I work. Hopefully this won't take but an hour or so, and if nothing else comes up, I should be able to finish up at the office another hour after that, and then head home. See what you can find for flights headed south out of both O'Hare and Midway. If you can find a late flight this evening, I can drive you to the airport. Otherwise, if you're flying out in the morning, you'll probably need to use Uber. If you want to fly all the way into Waco, you may have to wait until tomorrow morning. I don't know if they have any late flights from DFW into Waco, and I'd rather you fly all the way, instead of renting a car in Dallas and trying to drive south down I-35 on a Friday night. That traffic would be atrocious. Thanks again for being so understanding, and I'll see you this evening as soon as I can."

Chapter 23

Bill was about a block from Miller's when he got a text from Don Czerwinski. "Got a booth at Miller's. Sitting in the back with your plumber. Look for two guys wearing blue work shirts." Bill walked into the bar, let his eyes adjust to the lowered lighting level, and found the booth he wanted. There was already a half full pitcher of beer in front of the guys, and they didn't bother to stand up when Bill approached. The two in the booth were sitting across from each other, and one of them scooted in, making room for Bill.

"Hi! I'm Bill. I'll buy the next pitcher." He shook hands with the two, and they introduced themselves. He caught the attention of a waitress, and pointed at the beer steins, held up two fingers, and then pointed at the pitcher, holding up one. The waitress nodded and headed for the bar. "I know you two want to know what's going on, but I would rather wait until Steve Jennings gets here to discuss the project. In the meantime, why don't you two fill me in on your backgrounds? You know I'm FBI, but I don't know anything about the two of you, except that Steve vouches for you."

Don spoke up first. "I've been a welder for about twenty years. I've worked on everything from the Willis Tower, which used to be the Sears Tower, to helping Geraldo Rivera open Al Capone's vault in the Lexington Hotel. You name it, I've probably worked on welding it.

Bill smiled. "Well, I might have a new one for you. Arnie, tell us about your background."

Arnie saluted. "I know Steve told you I used to be in the Marines. And once a Marine, always a Marine. The discipline they teach you has helped me throughout my life. I wouldn't have traded that experience for anything in the world. I've been a plumber for over fifteen years. This obviously has some sort of plumbing connection, or Steve wouldn't have invited me to this party. Like Don, who I've known for years, I can work on just about any sort of plumbing problem."

At that point the waitress showed up with their second pitcher of beer, and two more beer steins. Bill told her that they would run a tab, and she nodded. Bill poured himself a beer, emptying the first pitcher, and the waitress took it off the table. Everyone took a sip, and then Steve Jennings walked up to their booth. He sat down next to Arnie, and poured himself a beer, too.

Bill looked at each of them. "Okay, it's time to fill you in. First, I must swear each of you to secrecy. What I'm about to tell you has national security implications, and you can't talk about it to your coworkers, your family, or anyone else. If word leaks out, we could all be in some serious trouble. Steve has already agreed to these rules. Don, Arnie, are you okay with this?" The two tradesmen looked at each other, and then both nodded.

Bill continued. "Thanks for trusting me on this, not knowing what it was about. This is going to be hard to believe, but I'm giving you the straight poop. Terrorists have smuggled a bomb into Chicago. It is not an atomic bomb, but it is what is called an RDD – a Radioactive Dispersal Device. That means that if it goes off, it will spread radioactivity over several square blocks of downtown Chicago, making that area uninhabitable for years.

The good news is that we know where the bomb is located – in a storeroom in the basement of Steve's hotel. The bad news is in two parts. First, the bad guys have gotten people hired as staff at the hotel, and they are watching the bomb. If we try and evacuate, or call in the bomb squad, they claim they will just set off the bomb. The second part of the bad news is even worse. We want you guys to go in and help disarm the bomb, without anyone knowing we are working on it."

Don and Arnie just sat there, looking stunned. Steve grinned. "Yep, that was my first reaction when I heard about the bomb, too. But it's true, and we've got to do something about it. Bill's thought is that they brought in the bomb to use during the Republican Convention in a few weeks. But we don't want to wait that long. We want to go in tomorrow night, or actually early on Sunday morning, and disable the bomb."

Bill chimed back in. "The bomb was disguised as a Rheem Industrial Water Heater and put in the storeroom with a couple of real water heaters. That is where you two come in. We need a welder to help us take apart the water heater, and a plumber to help us understand what is a real part of the water heater, and what doesn't belong. Steve used to disarm bombs when he was in Iraq, so he will know what wires to cut and how to pull out the detonators safely. I'll be there with you, too. We have some work to do to get ready for this operation, which is why we're not going in there tonight. But we want to get the bomb disarmed as quickly as possible, just to make sure the bad guys don't decide to go ahead and set it off.

Don, we're going to need a portable welder, and something to capture the exhaust fumes in that storeroom – we don't want the room or the hallway leading to it smelling like exhaust fumes."

Don nodded. "I have a good portable welding system in a rack that rolls on two wheels, and a RoboVent machine that will capture the exhaust. I'll need someone to bring in that system, because I can't handle the welding equipment and the RoboVent at the same time."

Bill responded quickly. "No problem. We'll have people to help, or I'll do it myself. Arnie, besides your expertise, we need a

Rheem water heater shell we can leave in place of the bomb when we pull it out of the Hyatt. The idea is to have something there that looks like the bomb if someone is checking on it from time to time. We want to use that to try and lure the terrorist leader down to that storeroom to figure out why his bomb is not going off when he hits his remote button. We want to set a trap, and we need a Rheem shell to help make that work."

Arnie drummed his fingers on the tabletop for a moment. "I haven't pulled any out of service in the last few weeks, but I think I know where I can get us one. There is a shop here in town that refurbishes heaters. It is so expensive to buy a new one that used ones in good shape can make a plumber some money, too. Let me make a call tomorrow and see if they have something we can use. What are your plans for getting the bomb out of the building, and the fake bomb back into that storeroom?"

"I'm glad you reminded me. We need to borrow the cart you would use to bring a new water heater into the hotel. The bomb will probably weigh close to a thousand pounds, near what those water heaters weigh. We'll have enough help in the storeroom to get it on the cart after we get it disarmed, but we will still need the cart, because it will be heavy. Once we have it out of the hotel, and into the back of our van, we can take the Rheem shell back down to the storeroom using that same cart. Since water heaters don't come with handles, we may want some ropes to use to help pick up the fake heater, and then set down the shell after we get the bomb out of the way.

There is another issue we need to discuss. When we open the water heater, there is probably going to be some radioactivity leakage. We are all going to be exposed to some extent. We have a NES Team flying into Chicago this evening – that's a Nuclear Emergency Support Team, so saying NEST Team is redundant, but it is easier to say it that way – and they are bringing us protective clothing like aprons, gloves, and helmets to wear while we are in the storeroom. We will also be wearing radiation dosimeters, to tell us how much radiation we have absorbed. I THINK we will get a dose about like an X-ray, but I can't guarantee that, because I don't know how much radioactivity will leak when we open the water heater. Worst case scenario would be that you won't be able to have any more kids after this operation. We got a radioactivity hit on a Geiger counter up in Michigan where the terrorists worked on the bomb, but it was a low-level finding, so I'm thinking this will not be a major issue. If this is a serious issue with any of you, let me know now, so that we can find someone to replace you on the team."

All three guys looked at each other. "Damn," Arnie said. "I'm in." The other two chimed in with a "Me, too."

Bill looked at each one of them, staring into their eyes to try and measure their level of commitment. "Thank you" is all he said. Bill added Arnie's phone number to his list of contacts, gave Arnie his cell number, and they finished their beers.

Bill told them, "I'll be in touch with each of you tomorrow to iron out the details, but right now you can plan on meeting in the basement of the Federal Building at about 1:00 AM Sunday morning. We will suit up there, and head for the hotel. Steve will already be at the hotel and will make sure we have access to the loading dock, the freight elevator, and the storeroom. With luck, we will be in and out of there without anyone noticing anything out of the ordinary. If you think of any other issues we need to work out before this caper, call me immediately, day or night, so that we can keep things moving. Does anyone have any questions right now? If not, I've got to get back to the office." No one said anything, so Bill signaled the waitress and paid for the two pitchers of beer. "Okay, you guys are on your own after this – I'm not paying for beer that I'm not going to be here to help drink." Everybody laughed. Bill thought that it was good to hear that they could still laugh, under the circumstances.

Cindy had gone home when Bill got back to the office, but Melissa Anderson was still there. She hung up the phone in Bill's outer office just as he walked in. "Cameras are up and running, both in the stairwell and the elevator, and the walkie-talkie we gave Steve Jennings works fine from the storeroom. We have the van in place, monitoring the cameras. It's parked in the convention center parking garage. We thought that might draw less attention than if we put it in the hotel garage. You have calls to return to the Director and Randy Marshall in Dallas. The NEST group will be here in about an hour, but I told them to go on to the hotel and that you would meet with them in the morning. Our big van is ready for the bomb, with the seats removed and a cradle added to hold the bomb. Anything else before I head home?"

"Thanks, Melissa. You might want to stick around for the call with Randy Marshall. After all, you are the one that first came up with the idea that there might be a second bomb. Dallas wouldn't even have a clue if it wasn't for you." Melissa smiled at the compliment and followed Bill back into his office.

Bill dialed Randy's direct line in the Dallas office, and Randy picked up on the first ring. He didn't waste any time after he found that it was Bill on the line. "I don't know how you did it, but you were right. We have a bomb in the Omni, next door to our convention center, stored with other water heaters. The kicker here is that the Omni does not use Rheem heaters, so you would think that it would have stood out as an anomaly – but no one seems to have noticed. Maybe it hasn't been there that long. I've been trying to come up with a team capable of disarming our bomb, but I haven't had much luck. How about you?"

"First, I need to tell you that I have you on speaker, and Melissa Anderson is in here with me. She is the one that put two and two together when she saw the report about the fish box in Louisiana. So, you can thank her for figuring out that there were two bombs, and not just the one here in Chicago."

"Hi, Melissa. Great job figuring this out. Since this is kind of your bomb, maybe I ought to just turn this project over to you and go on vacation for a few weeks."

Both Bill and Melissa laughed. Melissa said, "Thanks, I think!"

Bill spoke up. "Randy, I just met with the team I'm going to use here to try and disarm our bomb. I got to thinking on my walk back to the office that if this works, maybe we should use the same bunch on your bomb, too. They will already have the experience, and things might be easier the second time around. I'm sure we could get a plane to fly everyone to Dallas once our bomb is disarmed and in the hands of NEST. I would have to ask them to volunteer, but I have a feeling that would not be a problem. What do you think?"

"Not a bad idea. Experience counts for a lot in my book. Let me run that one by the Director, and I'll get back to you. How quickly do you think we could get them down here?"

"Maybe as early as Monday. One guy on our team is a welder, and one is a plumber. Our disarmament guy is the hotel's chief engineer, who used to disarm IEDs in Iraq during the war. I don't know what their schedules are for next week, but I can find out. My thought is the sooner we get both bombs disarmed and gone, the better. We're hitting the Hyatt Sunday morning about 2:00 AM. The idea is to get in and out without being seen by those watching the bomb. If we succeed, I suggest something similar for the Omni operation.

We set up cameras in the freight elevator and the stairway that leads to the floor where our bomb is stored, to give us some warning if someone is headed our way while we are working in that storeroom. You might want to investigate room access at the Omni and see what you can arrange for an early warning system before we attack that bomb. The Director sent us a NEST, and I'm sure he'll do the same for Dallas, to take the bomb off our hands once we have it disarmed and out of the hotel. Are you any closer to finding the rednecks behind your bomb?"

"Nope. And my staff is getting frustrated as hell looking for them."

"What we're going to do here in Chicago is put a dummy water heater back in that storeroom, and see if we can entice our guy to come in and see why his remote doesn't work when he tries to set off the bomb. We can stake out the place during the convention, and hopefully nab him when he shows up to see if he can reset things or set it off manually. If you like the idea, feel free to use it in Dallas, too. You'll need to find a water heater shell that you can use as a prop. The plumber on our team tells me that there is a shop here in Chicago that refurbishes old water heaters, and our guy thinks he can get us a Rheem shell from that place. You might see if there is some similar type of operation in the Dallas area."

"Another good idea. Now I'm beginning to see why the Director put you in Chicago. Maybe it wasn't just your good looks." Both Bill and Melissa laughed, again. "Okay, let me get to work on seeing what we need to do to help your team succeed here in Dallas, assuming there is any team left after you get through with the Chicago bomb. Melissa, can you send me a list of everything you've had to do to make this work in Chicago? That would save us a lot of time, and that way hopefully we don't miss anything important. Let me know if there are any issues with getting your team headed this way, and let me know when to expect them. I'll get the Director to have a jet standing by for them at Midway whenever they are ready to head south. Thanks to both of you for your help. We may be able to pull this off after all. And once we have some time, I want to hear the story of how you figured out they were using fake water heaters for the bombs. Great detective work on that one. Talk to you later."

Bill hung up and turned to Melissa. "Okay, get that list together, and send it to Randy. Then go home. I'm going to call the Director, and then hopefully I'll be right behind you. You're doing a fantastic job as acting Assistant Special Agent in Charge, and I couldn't ask for a better number two. Knowing Randy, he's going to offer you a promotion if you want to go to Dallas – but I'm going to try and find a way to keep you here if at all possible."

Melissa nodded, and headed for the door. Then she turned and looked back at Bill. "You know, even if Chet comes back, I doubt they would give him his old position, considering. So, there might be an opening here, too. Just keep that in mind!" Bill grinned at her chutzpah as she headed back to her desk.

He dialed the Director's office, not surprised to find him still there late on a Friday evening – even later since Washington was on Eastern time. FBI agents were dedicated people. As in any organization, there were always a few who thought that the required forty-four hours per week were pushing things a little too far, and who tried to skate when they could. But those people tended to get weeded out pretty quickly. Almost every agent Bill knew put in far more hours than required. It sometimes played havoc with family life – FBI agents have one of the highest divorce rates of any group of government servants – but agents cared, and it showed. And the Director led the way.

"Bill Peterson here in Chicago, Mr. Director. I'm just calling to let you know we have our disarmament team assembled, and we should be ready to go in early on Sunday morning, as we discussed. We think we have a pretty good plan, including setting up a trap for our terrorist, and I'll be happy to go over it in detail if you would like."

"No need. I trust you."

"I don't know if you have talked to Randy Marshall, but he has located his bomb, too. Same M.O. I suggested we use our team from Chicago to disarm their bomb, too. It might hold things up in Dallas for a day or two, but after our team takes apart the bomb here, I think that experience would expedite things in Dallas. What are your thoughts?"

"I don't like having to wait on disarming the Dallas bomb, but I think you are probably right on using the same team. Let me know what you need to get them to Dallas as soon as you can. Hopefully Sunday afternoon after you turn your bomb over to NEST, but no later than Monday. If that timetable doesn't work, we will have to look at using somebody else in Dallas. You okay with that?"

"Yes, sir. We'll get them to Dallas as soon as possible. I haven't discussed doing the second bomb with the team, but hopefully no one has any commitments early next week that they can't get out of. I'll let you know if there are any issues."

"Okay, let me know when NEST has your bomb. I doubt we will be putting out any press releases on it, at least until we get the Dallas bomb disarmed, too."

"Sir, I would rather you didn't. We want to use a fake bomb to try and lure in our terrorists both here and in Dallas, so we don't need to let them know that the real bombs are gone."

"Okay, your call. And if your traps work, we might consider some publicity at that time. 'FBI saves the conventions' doesn't sound too bad. Remember, I have to walk a political tightrope, too, and keep Congress happy. Publicity on disarming a couple of bombs would get me a lot of political capital. But we won't put anything out until either your traps work, or you find some other way to capture all these terrorists. Make sure nothing leaks from the people on your end. Talk to you on Sunday."

Bill thought to himself, "This has been a pretty good day. We're not there yet, but we made a lot of progress." He was whistling as he headed for his car. His good mood lasted until he got home to his condo, where he found a note from Julie. "Got an 8:30 flight out of Midway, with a quick connection at DFW on into Waco at midnight. Knew you were busy, so didn't want to bother you with the details. See you next week. Love you. And good luck this weekend!" Bill had thought he would have one more evening with Julie before she left for Texas, so his mood crashed when he read her note. He knew it was his fault – he had told her to go this evening if she could – but he was already missing her terribly. Not to mention that there wasn't anything worth eating in their fridge, and nothing good on television on Friday night. Oh, well. There was always Chinese that could be delivered, and he had a full briefcase of case notes to go over. The bomb was his highest priority, but there were lots of other cases being worked out of the Chicago office that needed his attention, too. He called for some sweet and sour chicken, with fried rice, and opened his briefcase to get to work.

Chapter 24

Saturday, May 30th

Bill stretched, and reached across the bed to put his arm around Julie. He woke up completely when he realized she wasn't there. He remembered her note, and promised himself he would find time to call her later this morning. He knew that today would be a crazy day, too, with everyone getting ready for Sunday. He decided no run today, so headed into the bathroom to shave and shower. His cell phone went off before he could duck into the water stream.

"This is Bill."

"Sir, this is Sargent Pascal at MCC. One of our Afghani prisoners was badly beaten last night, and is in our hospital ward. The other one is asking for you. Sounds like you've got another one willing to turn. I'm sorry to call you so early, but I wanted you to know about this before your day got too full. Want me to set something up like we did last time, so that you can talk to him?"

"Thanks for calling, Sargent. I appreciate the heads-up. I've got a lot on my plate today, but this is important, too. Let me see what I can work out, and I'll get back to you. Are you on shift all day today?"

"Yes, sir. I just came on at 6:00 this morning, and that's when I found out about Aarif. At least that's what we've been calling him – he refuses to even give us his name, but someone overheard his buddy say something to him, and the conversation included that name. We found him on the floor outside his cell in General Population, beat to a pulp. He nearly died before we could get some blood into him. Apparently, his buddy heard about the beating, and started hollering for you. We've already put the unharmed guy in isolation, just to protect him. He says his name is Abdul. Of course, no one saw or heard anything about the beating, and our cameras were conveniently turned away from that spot on the jail room floor. We're investigating that, too, but I doubt we'll come up with anything. Anyway, it looks like Aarif will live, and we may get something out of Abdul, so this one may end up as a win for us. Let me know when you think you can get out here, and we'll get you an interview room. What about Abdul's lawyer? Want me to contact him?"

Bill said, "Ask Abdul if he wants his attorney to be there when we talk. If Abdul will agree to talk without counsel being present, we may get more out of him. But if he says he wants his attorney there, we'll invite the shyster, too. I'll get back to you as soon as I can. Thanks again for letting me know about this stuff."

Bill pushed the "off" button on his cell phone, and finished his shower. Twenty minutes later he was on the way to his office, slowing only long enough to drive through Starbucks and grab his favorite cup of espresso. He figured he would need the caffeine and sugar, because that might be the only breakfast he would have time to consume.

He found the NEST leader waiting in his outer office when he arrived. Cindy pointed at Bill, saying, "Special Agent Peterson." The man stood up and Bill motioned for him to follow Bill into his office. "Sir, I'm Brownlee Washington, leader of the NES Team sent to take the bomb off your hands tomorrow morning. I've been fully briefed on the situation, and we're ready to help in any way possible. Our truck arrived early this morning, and we did bring the protective gear and dosimeters you asked for. If you want some of us going in with you, let me know. Otherwise, we'll stand off, and wait for you to come out with the bomb. All we need is a place to meet, to transfer the bomb from your van to our vehicle."

"Glad to have you here. One question, that I thought of last night. Is your vehicle marked as some sort of bomb disposal vehicle? We don't want something like that driving through our city streets, scaring people."

Washington shook his head. "No, sir. Somebody apparently thought of that years ago. Our trucks used to look like a city bomb squad truck, with 'danger' signs all over it. Someone finally realized that if we were carrying an atomic bomb, and it went off, staying a hundred yards back from our truck would not make any difference. Now, if you look closely at the back end, you'll see a small 'U.S. Government' logo, but nothing that even identifies the truck as belonging to a

NEST. We do have additional lead sheathing in our truck, including some pieces we can wrap around the bomb, if necessary, to help encapsulate whatever radioactivity is leaking. We won't know how bad that situation is until you get into the bomb and disarm it. We don't know how much, if any, you will have to penetrate the protective shell they have apparently already placed around the bomb. We know there was some leakage in that garage in Michigan, and some in the truck used to transport the bomb to Chicago, but how much worse that will be after you get into the works of the bomb are still to be determined.

We also have a pressure washer and some strong solvent available on our truck. We'll want anyone that comes in contact with the bomb to completely strip down and get blasted by our hose. We'll take whatever clothing you were wearing with us to be destroyed, so everyone on your disarmament team will need to have a change of clothes available, and we'll keep that set of clothing away from the bomb to make sure those clothes stay radiation-free. So, wherever we set up to do the transfer, we'll be better off if we have a little privacy. Maybe the city can give us a city park we can use early on Sunday morning, and help us to keep people out while we're doing our thing?"

"I know the Chicago Chief of Police. Let me contact him, and see what he suggests as a rendezvous point. I'm sure he knows what locations would work better than I do. He knows about the bomb, so I'm sure he will be willing to help. And thanks for the suggestions. This is your area of expertise, so any ideas on how to make our plan better will be gratefully accepted."

Washington nodded, and headed back to his team. He knew when he had been dismissed. Bill picked up his office phone. "Cindy, would you see if Glenn Simpson is in his office on a Saturday morning?"

Bill's phone buzzed thirty seconds later. Glenn didn't waste any time. "Of course, I'm in my office on a Saturday morning. Saturday mornings follow Friday nights, which are our busiest night of the week. We have more shootings on any given Friday night than Phoenix had in a month. What can I do this week for the FBI? Found our bomb, yet?"

Bill cut him off. "Are you alone in your office?"

"Yep."

"Yes, we found our bomb. It's in a storeroom at the Hyatt Regency McCormick Place. But we have a major problem. Allegedly the bad guys have people on staff at the Hyatt, watching for unusual activity. If we send in the bomb squad or try and evacuate the place, supposedly they are going to call the terrorist with the remote, and he is going to go ahead and set off the bomb.

Glenn blurted, "Jesus. And I thought I was already having a bad day."

Bill continued. "We have a plan to go in tonight and try and disarm the bomb, and get it out of the hotel. If everything works right, we'll be turning the bomb over to a NES Team sometime around four or five o'clock Sunday morning. What we need from you is a place for that turnover. The NEST guy tells me that everybody that has come in contact with the bomb will have to strip down and get hit with a pressure washer and solvent, while the NES Team guys load the bomb into their disposal vehicle. So, I'm thinking maybe a city park somewhere that you could block off for a few hours, to give us some privacy while we take our early morning showers? Not to mention that we don't want any publicity about the transfer taking place. My plan is to put a fake bomb in place of the real one, to try and catch our terrorist coming in to try and fix things when he realizes that his remote is not working, during the convention. So, no TV trucks, and no press releases about how the Chicago Police Department assisted the FBI with finding and removing a bomb from downtown Chicago – at least until after we get a chance to try and catch this guy. Capisce?"

"Do you need a firetruck to help wash everybody down?"

"Nope. The NES Team brought in their own pressure washer, so we can keep the people in the know to a minimum. And one more thing. There is another bomb in Dallas, awaiting the Democratic National Convention. If we successfully disarm our bomb tonight, we'll be flying the same team to Dallas to try and take apart their bomb, too. So that's another reason for you to help us keep things quiet. What's your thought on where we can set up this operation?"

Glenn thought for a moment. "About a half mile north from McCormick Place, past Soldier Field, is a road that leads around the Field Museum and goes out to the Adler Planetarium on Northerly Island. There shouldn't be anything going on out there at four AM on a Sunday morning. I'll make sure some of our guys have the keys to the gate that blocks that road, and we'll make sure you don't have any company. There will be a few guards around the Museum that might wonder what's going on, so we'll have to make up a story about some sort of training exercise to satisfy their curiosity. The Planetarium parking lot would make a great spot for your bomb transfer and for everybody getting a shower. Just don't get too close to the beach, or you might be spotted by somebody in a boat offshore. I'd hate for us to get a call about naked people at the Planetarium. If that went out on the police band, you would have a dozen reporters and television people there within fifteen minutes. So, keep your team out of sight of the beach. And call me on my cell when this is over. I'll sleep better once that bomb is out of Chicago."

Bill said, "Thanks, Glenn. I owe you another one." They hung up and got back to work.

Bill filled in the NES Team leader, and he sent some people to check out the site, to make sure it would work. As Washington was walking out of Bill's office for the second time, Bill's cell phone rang. "Bill? This is Arnie Razolli. I've found us a Rheem water heater shell we can use as our dummy bomb. But this bunch wants $500 for it. Are you going to authorize that expense? I can pay for it, and then bill you, but I wanted to make sure I was going to get my money back before I bought the thing."

"The government is good for it. I'll get you paid back, if I must pay for it myself, but I think we can justify that expense. Do you want me to give them my credit card number?"

"No need, they'll give it to me on a thirty-day credit, just adding it to my account. Okay, I'll load it in my truck. Let me know when and where you want to meet, to transfer it to your FBI van."

"I'm working on that right now. We're probably going to do that transfer in the parking garage here at the Federal Building, somewhere around midnight tonight, so that there won't be too many prying eyes around here, either. And while I have you on the phone, I've got another question for you. I don't know if I told everybody last night, but there is a second bomb, in a similar hotel in Dallas. I'm thinking we may want to use this same team to disarm that second bomb, too, because you guys will have the experience of working on the first one. What are your plans for the first part of this coming week? If we flew you to Dallas, would you be willing to work on the second bomb, too? Of course, you would be on the clock for all of this, so if we don't get blown to smithereens you stand to make a load of money out of this deal. What do you think?"

Arnie paused. "I don't have any jobs that I can't put off, or give to one of the other plumbers on staff. I can make myself free for the whole week, if you need me. Will we need a second Rheem shell for Dallas?"

"Thanks, Arnie. I really appreciate you volunteering. Yes, we will probably need a second Rheem shell, but we can probably get that somewhere in Dallas. I've got my Dallas counterpart checking for used water heaters in that area. Okay, plan on meeting me in the basement of the Federal Building a little before midnight, tonight. There is a gate on the doorway to the garage, and you need a passkey to get in, but I'll have somebody at the gate who can let you in. Just tell them you're with me if they ask. And bring a second set of clothing and shoes. The NES Team tells me they will have us strip down and hit us with a pressure washer to make sure they get any residual radioactivity off of us after we give them the bomb – so we need to get this done and us out of the hotel while it is still dark."

Since the team was fresh on Bill's mind, he decided to go ahead and call Don Czerwinski, the welder. Don picked up on the fourth ring. "Don't you know what time it is, and that it's Saturday morning?"

Bill laughed. "Rise and shine, sleepy head. We have work to do. Do you want to see a Rheem before we get to the hotel tonight, just to familiarize yourself with what you'll be working with? Arnie has found a Rheem shell, and he's picking it up now. What do you think?"

Bill could hear the yawn coming through the phone before Don answered. "No need. I've rewelded water heaters before, so I don't see a need to see this one in advance. I do have a couple of questions, but they are probably ones Steve will have to answer. I'll need electricity for the RoboVent. Do I need to bring an extension cord? And is there an available outlet in that storeroom? I'm assuming there is, but we need to make sure before we hit that door. And how much time will we have to get this done? The secret to breaking the weld on the water heater will be to provide enough heat to loosen the weld, without heating it to the point that it sets off the explosives. So, we will have to take it slow and easy as we try and get into the heater. Will we have enough time?"

Bill responded, "I'll check with Steve on outlets and an extension cord. He is my next call. As to time, we plan to meet at midnight in the basement garage here at the Federal Building, and then head to the Hyatt. I think you will have several hours if you need that much time. I'd like to be out of the hotel by four AM or so, just to give us time to make the bomb transfer to the NES Team guys while it is still dark outside. Plus, they tell me we are all going to have to strip down and get hit with a pressure washer after we work with the bomb, just to make sure we don't have any radioactive dust stuck to us. So, bring an extra set of clothes and shoes, and wear something to work on the bomb that you probably won't get back.

And I've got a question for you. I don't know that I mentioned it last night at the bar, but there is a second bomb in a hotel in Dallas, with bad guys there planning on setting it off during the Democratic National Convention. I'm thinking that if we are successful at disarming this bomb, you guys would have a much better chance of disarming that second bomb, too. How would you feel about a trip to Dallas? Do you have anything planned for this coming week that you can't get out of? I know I'm asking for a quick decision, but we're trying to make plans on how to get that bomb disarmed, too, and you guys are going to be the experts after this first go-round. What do you think?"

Don didn't hesitate. "No problem. I'll be happy to help. When would we be heading for Dallas?"

"Thanks, Don. I really appreciate you volunteering. We'll probably head south late Sunday evening, or early Monday morning. We want to get to that bomb as quickly as possible, too. But you guys are going to need some sleep after our Saturday night/Sunday morning soiree. So, my guess is head to Dallas Monday morning, and we may hit that hotel Monday night or early Tuesday morning. Arnie has already agreed to go, and like I said, my next call is to Steve Jennings. My guess is that the FBI will provide us with a private plane out of Midway, so there won't be any problem bringing whatever equipment you need. Call me if you have any questions. Otherwise, I'll see you at midnight in our basement garage. I'll have somebody at the gate to make sure you can get in."

Bill hung up and immediately called Steve Jennings. Steve picked up on the first ring. "Hello?"

"Steve, this is Bill Peterson. I've got several things to discuss with you. Are you alone?"

"Yep. I'm still at home, and I live alone."

"Good. First, after thinking it over, I'm not sure it is a good idea for you to stay at the Hyatt tonight. Someone might see you going in or out of your room, and that would raise some flags. Plus, I've been told by our NES Team guys that they will want to give everyone a shower with a pressure washer when we come off the hotel property, to make sure we are not carrying any residual radioactivity somewhere on our clothes or skin. So, you'll need to bring a second set of clothing with you, and don't plan on getting your first set back from NEST. I think it would be better if you came in with the rest of the team through the loading dock, and then left when we leave. What do you think?"

"Makes sense to me. I'll tell my boss that she just saved the cost of that steak dinner."

"Hah. I'll buy you that steak dinner when this is all over. And that brings up my second point. I don't think I mentioned it when we were at lunch or in the bar with Arnie and Don, but there is a second bomb at a hotel in Dallas, ready to go off during the Democratic Convention. How would you feel about a trip to Dallas after we disarm this bomb? My thought is that our team will have the experience after the first one, which would make it safer to use the same people on the Dallas bomb. Once we get that bomb disarmed, I'll buy you the biggest steak you can find at any Dallas steakhouse. Can you get free this next week? Are you willing to go after the second bomb, too?"

"Yeah, I'm willing to go to Dallas, as long as the rest of the team is willing. Us working on both bombs does make sense. Are we going to have to sneak into that hotel, too? Which hotel in Dallas?"

"Thanks, Steve. I appreciate you volunteering. Both Arnie and Don have already agreed to go, too. The hotel is the Omni in Dallas. I'm sure their setup is probably like yours here, but we'll have people researching that situation, so we know what we're getting into when we hit that hotel. My guess is that we'll fly by private plane from Midway sometime on Monday morning, and maybe hit the Omni Monday night or early on Tuesday. We want to get that bomb disarmed as quickly as possible, too. We'll have their hotel engineer available to brief all of us when we hit Dallas.

As for tonight, the rest of the team is going to meet at midnight here in the parking garage at the Federal Building. Do you want to meet us here? Or would you rather meet us at the gate to the back dock at the Hyatt?"

Steve thought for a moment. "I think it would make sense for all of us to ride together. Too many vehicles around the hotel late at night might raise some suspicions. I can jump out at the gate and use my passkey to get that vehicle into the parking lot. It would probably be better if they let us all out on the dock, and then left. I don't want them parked at the dock in the middle of the night. I can give your driver my passkey, so that he can get back in when it is time to come pick all of us up and get the bomb."

"That makes sense. We'll set it up that way. Okay, next couple of questions are from Don. He wanted to make sure there was an available electrical outlet in that storeroom where the bomb is located, and whether or not he needed to bring an extension cord to plug in his RoboVent – that's the machine that hopefully will suck up the smell from the welding. What do you think?"

Steve said, "We have plenty of outlets, but it would probably be a good idea to bring an extension cord. I don't know how long the cord is that comes with the RoboVent, so just to make sure I would bring an extension."

"Okay, see you tonight at midnight. And make sure Lisa knows to cancel your room reservation, if you made one."

"I'll have to cancel the reservation. If I know Lisa, she is going to be as far from Chicago as she can get this weekend. I think this bomb has her frightened so badly she can't walk."

Bill said, "I understand. Some people react that way. I'm glad you've got a cool head on your shoulders. We'll need that tonight. See you at midnight."

Bill called Don back, and told him to bring an extension cord. "Other than that, I think everybody knows what we need. I'll probably have Melissa Anderson, my number two, follow up with everyone this afternoon just to make sure we are all on the same page."

Bill called Randy Marshall in Dallas, and told him that the team had all volunteered to help disarm the Omni bomb, too. Randy told him that things were getting set up in Texas, and that the Dallas office would be ready for the bomb disarmament team when they arrived.

Bill looked at his "To Do" list on his phone, and found that he had a few hours free. He decided he had time to get out to MCC and see what the Afghani had to say – every bit of information could make a difference on safely disarming the bomb. Bill called Sargent Pascal at MCC, and asked him to set up an interview room. "I should be there in about thirty minutes, assuming traffic isn't too bad this early on a Saturday morning."

"Yes, sir. We'll have Abdul waiting. He says he is willing to talk to you without his lawyer in the room, so that may help. See you shortly."

Bill headed for the Metropolitan Correctional Center.

Chapter 25

Abdul was led into the interrogation room in shackles, and then handcuffed to a ring in the floor. He looked very disheveled. Bill asked him, "Are you okay?"

Abdul shook his head no. "I'm scared. If the guards put me back in GenPop, I'm going to end up like Hamid, or dead. I'd rather take my chances with the government."

Bill looked him in the eyes. "If I find out you're lying to me about anything, I'll make sure the gangs in GenPop not only know where to find you, but that you're a snitch, too. How long do you think you would last under those circumstances?"

"I'll tell you the truth! I promise! What do you wish to know? I can tell you that it was the Iranians behind all of this. Hezbollah recruited the two of us from Kandahar, because of our bomb making expertise. They sent us to a camp in Syria, but it was the Iranians that were running the camp. They told us that they had a way to smuggle us into the United States, along with the bomb.

They had a second bomb, and they said it was going to Dallas. Are you aware of that bomb? All we had to do was to finish setting up the bomb when we arrived. They showed us how to fit the bomb into the water heater shell, and then how to connect the batteries and the remote-control device. It's really a pretty simple bomb – they could have done it without our expertise.

The boat that took us from Canada to meet the U.S. boat was captained by a naturalized Canadian citizen, but he was originally from Iran. He said his cousin was an undersecretary at the Iranian Embassy in Canada, and that the cousin arranged all the smuggling trips into the United States. I can give you names, dates, anything you want! Just help me! Please!"

"Do you know where Mohammed is staying?"

"No, sir. I do not. He did not tell us where he was going. I'm sorry, but I can't help you there. I would tell you if I knew, but I don't have a clue."

"Are you willing to make a statement about everything you know about Iranian involvement, from the time you were recruited, until you were captured? Would you be willing to be interviewed by someone from the United States State Department?"

"Yes, sir. Whatever you need. Just keep me out of GenPop."

This was the first Bill had heard about Iranian involvement, and he knew he was in over his head on this one. "Okay, we'll put you in isolation. I want you to spend an hour a day here with Sargent Pascal, with him recording everything you can remember about your recruitment, trip to Syria, and the trip to the United States. I want names, dates, locations, travel methods, anything you can think of. I'll get someone here to continue this interview. Right now, I have to get back to work. But you can start working with Sargent Pascal. If you balk at releasing any information, or if you refuse to answer any of his questions, or any questions from the State Department, I'll hear about it – and you won't like the consequences. So be honest and thorough. I want you to know I'm not doing this for your best interest – I'm doing this for the United States of America. So, listen to the Sargent carefully, answer all his questions, and we may just be able to keep you alive. Sargent, he's all yours."

Bill called the Director on his way back to the office from the MCC. "Sir, you may not believe this one. One of the Afghans we captured with our SWAT Team raid broke, and started giving us information. The other Afghan got beat up badly last night, so this guy, named Abdul, is pretty scared. He says he and the other guy were recruited by Hezbollah, and that the Iranians are the ones that smuggled them, and the bombs, into the U.S. He says he is willing to give names and dates and places to whomever we want to send to interrogate him, as long as we keep him out of reach of the gangs in MCC. I thought the North Koreans were behind the bombs, but now this guy brings up Iranian involvement. Is it possible we have two state actors involved in trying to blow up our national conventions?"

"Interesting. We don't have much on North Korean involvement, other than that email account starting point. Plus, I wondered how the NPRK managed to handle the smuggling - I didn't know they had those kinds of contacts. So maybe we do have two different foreign states helping to bring weapons of mass destruction into the United States, or maybe it was just the Iranians all along. I'll have to think about this one. Do you want some help with the interrogation?"

"Yes, sir. I'm afraid this is way over my level of expertise. We may need someone from the State Department, or even the CIA to help interrogate this guy and wring him dry. I can use whatever help you can get me. Not to mention that we need to figure out how to verify his story, to make sure he isn't just feeding us a line of B.S. So please send me somebody that can handle this level of intrigue."

"Okay, good work getting this guy to open up. Let me talk to the Secretary of State, and see who we can get to Chicago. I doubt State has anyone currently in Chicago that could handle that level of information, but I'm sure they'll be happy to help, and we'll get someone there as quickly as possible. Anything new on the bombs?"

"We're going in tonight to disarm the Chicago bomb, and everyone on the team has agreed to fly to Dallas and work on that bomb, too. I'll need a plane Monday morning at Midway to get us to Dallas."

"I'll handle that," the Director said. "We'll have a plane at an FBO at Midway by 8:00 Monday morning. I'll let you know which Fixed Base Operator we will be using. Good luck tonight. Be careful. Anything else you need?"

"No, sir. We're good to go. Thanks for all of your assistance."

"No problem. Believe it or not, support is probably half of my job. You keep doing great work, and maybe you'll find out for yourself one day."

That was about the nicest thing Bill had ever heard from the Director, and he had a hard time keeping his mind on the road. As usual, the Director had hung up without saying goodbye. Bill was beginning to realize that the Director made that a habit, to save a few seconds on every call.

Next, Bill called Julie in Waco. "Hi, sweetheart, how are you? How was your trip to Texas?"

"I'm fine. It's a lot warmer down here – already over ninety degrees during the afternoons. The flight down was tiring, but I made it okay. How are things in Chicago?"

"We're going in to try and disarm our bomb tonight. If that works, we're going to fly to Dallas on Monday, and work on getting that bomb disarmed, too. Probably Monday night. So, if you wanted to wait until Tuesday or Wednesday to head back north, we could probably fly back together, if you want some company. Would your Mom be willing to put me up, too, for a night or two if I came on south from Dallas to Waco, after we finish our business in Dallas?"

"I'm sure she would be happy to see you, too.   Are you sure you want to work on the Dallas bomb? Couldn't someone else take on that one?"

"We could get someone else to do it, but it makes sense for our team to try. After we do the first one, we'll have the experience, and that should make the second one go quicker and easier. I know you don't like having me in harm's way, but I feel like I can contribute."

"Okay, be careful. I'll see you when, then? On Tuesday?"

"Yep, probably on Tuesday. We should be going after the Dallas bomb early on Tuesday morning, so as soon as that's over, and I get a few hours sleep, I'll rent a car and drive on south to Waco. Okay, I'm back at the office, and have to get off the phone. Love you!"

"Love you, too. Bye."

Bill spent the afternoon meeting with his staff, making sure everyone was on the same page. The team watching the stairwell and elevator reported no one paying any attention to the storeroom where the bomb was located. The van driver got his instructions. An agent was appointed to be the gate keeper at the Federal Building on Saturday night, to make sure everyone that needed to could get into the parking garage. The NES Team leader, Brownlee Washington, was told about the midnight rendezvous, and he promised to have his team there with the protective gear, so that Bill's team could get suited up before heading for the hotel. Washington told Bill that his team had checked out the planetarium parking lot, and they agreed that is was a perfect place to do the bomb handoff and get the team hosed down. Melissa Anderson told Bill that she had double checked with everyone on the team about what equipment was needed, and everyone knew what to bring. She had also developed a list of what everyone needed, and had sent that to Randy Marshall in Dallas. The stuff they used in Chicago would end up being possibly contaminated by radioactivity, and would be turned over to NEST to be destroyed. They would need a new set of everything to tackle the Dallas bomb.

Bill thought that they had developed a pretty good plan. Now all they had to do was execute it without any mistakes.

Chapter 26

Sunday, May 31st

Bill actually got to the parking garage about 11:30 Saturday night, before midnight, expecting to be the first to arrive. But he found the NES Team already there, laying out the protective gear everyone going into the hotel was supposed to wear. They had a lightweight overcoat type sheath that zipped up the back and covered the body from the neck to the ankles. There was room to walk in it, but that was about it. The sheath had long sleeves, with connections for gloves that used Velcro to attach to the arms of the sheath. There was also a helmet, and booties with traction on the bottom of the slippers to wear over their shoes. With all the gear on, it was going to be hard to work on the bomb – but the gear was necessary to protect the team from radioactivity exposure. There was a dosimeter for each person, to be worn under the sheath.

As Bill suited up, he commented to Brownlee that, "We better hope no one sees us in this gear. Either we're going to scare the hell out of someone, or they'll think a UFO has landed in Chicago." Washington laughed. "Yeah, you should see the doubletakes we get when we're running a drill and some unsuspecting bystander sees us in our gear. I've seen people actually drop whatever they were holding, and run for the hills."

Agent James Rollings, from Bill's staff, was next to show. "I understand you needed someone with some brains on the team?" was his only comment as he started getting in his protective gear. Bill told him, "The bomb probably weighs around a thousand pounds. We'll need everyone of your "brains" to help with this one. It probably wouldn't be a good idea to drop the bomb while we were trying to load it or carry it out of the hotel." Rollings laughed.

Next was Arnie Rizzoli, the plumber. The NES Team helped him pull the water heater shell out of Arnie's van, and put it into the FBI van. They also loaded the cart that would be used to transport the water heater in, and the bomb out of the hotel. Arnie looked at all the protective gear, and said, "When I was a kid, I wanted to be an astronaut. Now, I guess I get to see what that feels like." Bill told him, "Don't plan on getting that cart back. It will probably glow in the dark after we're done moving the bomb with it."

Steve Jennings pulled into the garage. "I took a chance, and drove by the hotel. Still a few late-night revelers wandering in through the front of the hotel, and a few cars headed into our parking garage, but the backside of the place looked quiet. We might want to wait until after two AM to hit the place, just to make sure all the people helping to close the bars get back to the hotel before we go in through that back gate."

Bill told him, "I'm not sure we can wait that long, because we have to be back out and get the bomb transferred before it gets to be daylight, and that comes pretty early up here this time of year. We can have somebody monitoring the front of the hotel while we are going in, just to make sure no one will be spotting us." Bill got on his walkie-talkie, and talked to the people in the van watching the hotel cameras. "Can you spare somebody to watch the front of the hotel? We want to make sure we're not interrupted while we're going in the back gate. We'll probably be hitting the gate around one AM, so if you can get someone in place a little before that it would help."

"No problem, sir. We're on it."

The last team member to arrive, Don Czerwinski, didn't get to the hotel parking lot until almost 12:30 AM. "Sorry I'm so late. Would you believe I forgot to put an extension cord in the back of my truck, and had to go back to the shop to get one?"

Bill told him, "No problem. Glad you are here with everything you need." The rest of the team helped Don load his equipment in the back of the FBI van, and then Don got help from the NES Team getting his gear on.

Bill gave them one last quick pep talk. "Okay, guys, I think we're as ready as we're going to be. You all know what needs to be done, and we need to do it as quietly and efficiently as possible. I'll be monitoring the radio communications from our van, and if they spot somebody coming down the stairs or the freight elevator at the hotel, they'll let me know through my blue tooth earpiece, and I'll let you know we need to shut everything down and be perfectly quiet until that person leaves. James, you'll be responsible for shutting down the RoboVent. If necessary, pull the plug. I'll get the light switch when everything else is shut down, and I'll stay by the door in case someone tries to come into the room. The rest of you, if I signal, don't waste any time shutting off all your equipment. We want to be sitting in a dark room, everyone being still and quiet, with the lights off and the door locked, if anyone wanders down that hallway. We'll take Arnie's dummy water heater in with us as we go. We just want to make one trip in and out, if possible, so all the equipment and the fake water heater needs to go in, and then all the equipment and the bomb needs to come out on a single trip. It will be a rough go getting the bomb out of there along with all the equipment, so if there is an issue, some of the equipment may have to stay in that storeroom. Getting the bomb out takes priority over everything else, except for whatever we have to do to keep it from exploding. I've got faith in all of you. We can do this. Now, let's go."

Everyone piled into the back of the FBI van, except for Steve Jennings, who rode up front with the driver. The helmets the NES Team had provided had built in blue tooth earbuds, so everyone was able to communicate. As they approached the hotel, Bill called his lookouts. "Everything clear at the hotel?"

"You're good to go. No activity at all around the back side of the place. You can hit the gate."

The van pulled up to the gate, Steve hopped out, and used his passkey to open the gate. It slowly slid open, taking way too long in Bill's opinion. Finally, they were able to drive through. Steve just walked from the gate to the loading dock. Bill asked him, "Will the van have any trouble getting back out of the gate?"

"Nope. There is a pressure switch in the ground inside the gate there that automatically opens the gate when a vehicle hits the switch. But while I'm thinking about it, let me give him my gate key so that he can get back in when it is time to pick us up."

They started unloading equipment onto the loading dock, putting the water heater shell onto the cart that Arnie had provided. That shell didn't weigh too much, so that cart could be pushed with just one guy. James took that role. Arnie had his tools in a backpack. Don put the extension cord over his shoulder, and raised the handle on his portable welder, which was on wheels. Don's supplies were also in a backpack, and Bill decided he would take that. The RoboVent was also on wheels, so it could be pushed, too. Steve took that. They all headed for the freight elevator.

"Camera crew, any activity inside that we need to worry about?"

"No, sir. Quiet in the elevator and stairway."

Steve used his passkey to summon the freight elevator, and they all stepped inside. Even as big as the freight elevator was, it was crowded with five guys and all the equipment they were carrying. Bill warned them one more time. "Be careful getting out of the elevator. We don't want any noise from this point forward, if possible. Keep your equipment from banging against the walls."

Steve pushed the button for the basement level where the storeroom was located, and the elevator headed down. The elevator door opened onto a hallway, and Steve pointed to the left. They all turned that way. About half-way down the hallway Steve paused at a door, and used a regular door-type key to open it. He reached in and turned on the light, and they were in. Bill locked the door behind them.

There were three Rheem water heaters stacked near the back wall of the storeroom, all laying on their sides. Steve pointed at the one closest to the wall, and whispered, "This is the fake." Bill and Steve pushed the real water heaters away from the bomb, to give the team a little more room to work. Arnie started taking tools out of his backpack, to get started taking the top off the water heater. Don started setting up his welder. James asked, in a quiet voice, "Where do you want the RoboVent?"

"Set it up near the top of the water heater for right now. Once Arnie gets the top off, I expect to have to cut through the pressure seal into the guts of the heater." James plugged in the vent, and moved it into place. Arnie had a portable drill with a socket wrench attachment, and he started undoing screws around the top of the heater. Two minutes later he was done, and he was able to pull the top of the heater away from the rest of the mechanism, with James assisting him in lifting the heavy lid.

Bill asked Arnie, "Okay, what doesn't belong? What should Steve be looking for?"

"These two batteries shouldn't be here. This one has wires leading down toward the LED display, but this other battery is connected to this little box, that also doesn't belong. Maybe that's the remote control for the bomb? There are wires leading from that down into the bomb itself, so maybe that's connected to the firing mechanism, down below the pressure plate. Steve, what do you think?"

Steve looked over the mix of wires, boxes, and pump equipment in the top section of the water heater. "I think we can safely cut the wires to both batteries, and then start removing stuff. It doesn't look like they booby trapped anything, so I think it is a pretty simple setup, and hopefully we can disarm it pretty easily."

They all looked at Bill. He looked back at each of them, and finally just said, "Do it."

Steve took out a pair of wire cutters, and grabbed the wires from the battery to the remote receiver. He cut those, and then cut the wires from the receiver leading down into the guts of the heater. He then moved to the other battery, and cut the wires leading away from that battery, too. Nothing exploded, except for everyone's breath – it turns out they had all been holding their breath while Steve cut the wires. "Okay, now we need to remove the batteries and the receiver. Arnie, you see the brackets holding the batteries in place? Do you think you can get in there with your socket wrench and undo the nuts holding down those brackets? Arnie nodded, and went to work. He did it slowly and carefully, but five minutes later Steve could lift out the batteries and the receiver.

Steve turned to Don Czerwinski. "Okay, Don, you're up. We need the plate removed between the pump section and the heater section of the cylinder. But don't overheat it. Remember that there is probably a half ton of explosives under that plate."

Don automatically reached up to lower his face shield, but then remembered that he was already wearing a helmet. He lit his welder, and slowly started cutting a groove around the outside edge of the plate on the water heater. James turned on the RoboVent, so that it could start sucking up the fumes and smoke from the welder flame. It was a bit noisy, but that couldn't be helped – they had to eliminate those fumes, if they were going to be able to breathe, and even to see through the smoke. This model of vent had a hose attachment, so James was able to hold the hose close to where Don was cutting. The vent's vacuum seemed to be working well, as there wasn't much smoke escaping into the rest of the room.

Don was about half-way through his cut when Bill got a warning through his earpiece. "Shut it down. Someone is headed down the back stairs, and may be coming your way. Bill tapped Don on the shoulder, and when Don turned, Bill slashed his hand across his throat, signaling to cut things off. Arnie and Steve backed off a couple of steps, and James turned off the RoboVent. Don cut off his flame, and the room got quiet. Bill quickly moved to the door, turned, made a "shh" motion with his fingers to his lips, and then turned off the light. All they could do now was hope that whoever was coming did not have a key, and wouldn't smell the residue from the welding from air escaping under the door.

Two minutes later they could hear footsteps, and then someone rattled the doorknob. Bill was ready to turn on the light and take down the person investigating if they came into the room, but apparently the spy didn't have a passkey. A few seconds later they heard the footsteps retreating down the hallway. A couple of minutes passed, and then Bill heard, "You're clear. The guy just shut the door at the top of the stairs." Bill turned the light back on, and again it seemed like everyone had been holding their breath.

Don turned his welder back on, James turned on the vent, and they went back to work. Five minutes later, they were ready to peel back the plate. It was still hot from Don's cutting, so they grabbed the edges with a pair of pliers, and slowly lifted it out of the water heater.

Steve looked into the water heater, and said simply, "Wow." Sitting there were eight packets of plastic explosives, which Steve said were probably Semtex. They were wired in parallel, with the wires all leading back to the remote receiver location in the top of the heater. This wasn't the main part of the bomb – that was still in a lead sealed container below the Semtex. This was the charge that was to be used to detonate the rest of the bomb. Steve started lifting out the packets, one at a time, and handing them to James. He put them into a spare duffel bag he found in the corner of the storeroom. They had forgotten to bring something to use to carry out the bomb parts they removed from the bomb. Once the Semtex was removed, they could see the lead shield that separated them from the radioactive part of the bomb. Everybody looked at Steve.

"That's it?" Bill said. Steve nodded. "I think so. I think we can safely move the bomb."

Everybody slumped a little, relaxing from the tension. But then Arnie spoke up. "Wait a minute."

Bill looked at him. "What is it? Something still seem out of place?"

Arnie pointed at the LED display on the front of the water heater. "I don't like the looks of that display. Normally, the window is flush with the front of the heater, but this one sticks out about a half-inch. Look at what the display looks like on the other two heaters, and tell me what you think."

Don checked the other heaters. "Yeah, the windows are flush with the cylinder surface on these two. Maybe whoever designed the bomb had to push the LED display out to make room for the bomb shield?"

Arnie said, "Maybe. But I'm not sure. You told me to look for anything different, and this is different."

Bill looked at Don. "Can you cut a square about a foot on each side around that display, without messing with the display? Just to make sure, I think we need to see what's under that LED."

Don said, "No problem. James, crank that vent back up one more time." Don restarted his welder, and went to cutting. Ten minutes later the square was done, and they were able to grab the edges with a pair of pliers and peel it back from the heater. Steve took a flashlight, and shined it into the hole where the LED had been. "Why, you sneaky little devils!"

Bill said, "What are you seeing?"

"Whoever designed this added a second, manual way to set off the bomb. The LED display is really what we call a rocker or toggle switch. Your rock it back and forth, and then push it in, and it sets off a timer just underneath the display. There is a completely separate set of detonator Semtex packs in the opening behind the LED. Let me cut a couple of wires, and we'll have this area disarmed, too. I guess the designers figured that even if somebody disabled the remote control at the top of the bomb, this area would probably be overlooked, and the bomb could still be exploded. But thanks to eagle-eyed Arnie, we've seen through their scheme and totally disarmed the bomb."

Bill shook his head. "Good work, you guys. Do you think we need to take the bottom of the bomb off, too, just to make sure there is not a third way to set it off?"

Steve said, "I don't think so. It looks like the lead cylinder just fits into the water heater shell, except for the areas where the pumps were located at the top, and this area around the LED display. So, I think the bottom of the heater can be left alone."

Don added, "That bottom looks like where they opened the heater to get the bomb into the shell, and then rewelded it. I can see the welding work that was done, and it doesn't look like they did a very professional job. I agree with Steve. I think we're done once he pulls out that remaining Semtex."

Steve carefully cut the wires from the toggle switch to the timer, removed the switch, and then started pulling out Semtex packets. He told James, "Don't slip and fall on our way out, or we might all still end up out in the middle of Lake Michigan. You've got quite a load of explosives in that bag. It is supposed to take an electronic charge to set that stuff off, but I'm not sure I would want to take that chance."

Bill said, "The same thing goes for the bomb. There is still a lot of plastic explosives in that cylinder, so we need to be careful moving it out of here."

Arnie maneuvered his cart over next to the bomb, and everybody gathered around the water heater. They slipped their ropes under the heater. Bill said, "Okay, we're going to lift on three, raise the bomb a foot at a time, and slide it over onto Arnie's cart. Once we have it there, James, you and I will hold it in place, and Arnie and Don, you strap it down." Bill looked at everyone. "Ready? One, two, THREE!" They all grunted from the load as they lifted, but they managed to get the water heater over the edge of the cart, and set it down fairly gently. They strapped it to the cart, and they were ready to roll.

With James pushing, and Don and Bill guiding, they managed to slide the water heater out into the hallway without banging up against the walls. They gathered up the rest of their equipment, and headed for the elevator. Bill called for their ride, but spoke quietly. "We'll be on the dock in two minutes."

"Yes, sir. I'll be there. Need help loading the bomb?"

"Yes, please. The thing is heavier than we expected, and hard to handle. We can use all the help we can get to move it from the cart to the cradle in the back of the van."

The team got all the gear, and the bomb, loaded onto the freight elevator, and Bill checked for clearance one last time.

"Anything happening around the back dock, or the back gate to the hotel?"

"No, sir. You're cleared to load."

The elevator opened onto the back dock just as the van was backing up to the dock. The team loaded all the loose equipment into the front part of the van's interior, up against the seats where the driver and front seat passenger sat. The driver, already geared up in protective gear, helped the rest of the team move the bomb from the cart on the dock to the cradle in the van. It took quite an effort, since the floor of the van was lower than the loading dock, and with the cart the bomb was sitting about three feet higher than the dock. So, they had to gently lower it from the cart down to people standing between the dock and the van, and then people had to jump off the dock to help move the bomb on into the van, and onto the cradle that had been built to hold it. That took almost ten minutes, and Bill made a mental note to fix that issue when they went to Dallas. But eventually they were done. Everyone jumped into the van, they closed the back doors, and headed for the Planetarium parking lot. It was 4:08 in the morning, and they had about ninety minutes before the sun started coming up. But the bomb was disarmed, and out of the hotel. All-in-all, Bill thought, not a bad morning's work. He called the NES Team leader and told Washington that they were on the way to the Planetarium.

Bill told him about the disarmament, including finding the second set of detonators. "Pretty clean job, and we didn't have to get into the radioactive area of the bomb. ETA about ten minutes."

"We're ready for you. We'll take over with the bomb as soon as you get here. All you have to do is strip down, get hosed down, and then get dressed in clean clothes. We've got people here to drive everyone back to their cars and trucks at the Federal Building as you get cleaned up.   We'll also check your dosimeters, but I don't expect much exposure, if what you tell me about the lead shield around the bomb is correct."

Fifteen minutes later the bomb was in the NEST truck, and it was heading out of town. Bill didn't know where they were taking the bomb – whether it was going to a lab somewhere for dissection, or out to a desert in the western part of the country to be blown to pieces – but Bill was too tired to care. The bomb was leaving Chicago, and that was enough for him. NEST was also taking over the FBI van and all of the equipment in the van – so if the team was going to do a repeat performance in Dallas, they would need a new set of everything. Tools, welding equipment, protective gear, a truck to move the bomb, a water heater shell to put in place of the bomb, and so on. Bill knew that Melissa was on top of the list of necessities, and that she would have been working with Randy Marshall to make sure everything was available when they got to Texas.

The bath with the pressure washer was really a three-part affair. First, the victim was blasted from head to toe. Then a mix of astringent chemicals was added to the water, to help clean even better. And finally, a last rinse to try and get all the chemicals off the body. But there was always a smell remaining after that last rinse, so everyone planned on taking another shower as soon as they got home.

Bill gathered everyone together before they were ferried back to the Federal Building. "You all did great work tonight. And your reward is that we get to do it again, probably Monday night, in Dallas. So, go home, get cleaned up, and get some sleep. All you need to bring for our trip to Dallas is what you would pack for a short vacation – clothes, toiletries, and so on. Don't worry about equipment. We are going to get a clean set of everything when we get to Dallas. Your hotel reservations and all of your meals are going on a government credit card, so you don't even need much cash. The only things we can't put on the card are booze and any porno movies you rent in your hotel room." Everyone laughed. "You'll have to pay for that.

I'll see all of you at the Signature Fixed Base Operator, or FBO, at Midway at 9:00 Monday, tomorrow morning. The FBI is sending us a jet to fly us to Dallas. I hope you all smell a little better by then." They laughed again, and everyone piled into the vans the NES Team was using. Since there wasn't any traffic at that time on a Sunday morning, they were back at the Federal

Building ten minutes later. Five minutes after that everyone was heading home.

Except for Bill. He had some phone calls to make, so he headed upstairs to his office. To his surprise, he found Cindy and Melissa there, and Cindy handed Bill a cup of coffee as he walked in. "I thought you would be headed back up here, and I figured you could use this. I also need to tell you that you smell."

"Thanks, Cindy. You're a lifesaver. I've got several people to talk to. Let's start with Glenn Simpson. I always wanted to wake up a police chief at 6:00 on a Sunday morning. And Melissa, I want to see your list of equipment you've asked Dallas to provide. We're probably going to need to get a bigger truck, to save us from the problem we had this morning trying to get our bomb loaded into the van."

Bill's phone buzzed, and when he picked it up, he could hear Glenn's cell phone ringing. Glenn finally answered, after about ten rings. "Hello?" Bill heard in a very sleepy voice.

"Glenn? This is Bill Peterson. I just wanted to let you know that our bomb has been disarmed, and is on its way out of the

Chicago area. I just wanted to thank you for your help with your undercover operative, and with the guys watching the street behind the museum leading to the planetarium. We couldn't have done this without the help of the Chicago Police Department."

Glenn yawned into the phone. "And this couldn't have waited until a decent hour to be reported? When I get a call at 6:00 AM I expect it to be something earthshaking, like the Governor or Mayor has been shot. I appreciate the call, but next time try and wait until I've had my first cup of coffee." Bill laughed, and heard Glenn laughing with him. "Good job, Bill. I knew you could do it. Maybe there will be a place for you in the Union League, after all. Especially after I tell them how you saved the place."

"Please don't say anything, Glenn. We're still trying to use the bomb site as a trap for our terrorist, so we don't want word getting out that the bomb is gone. At least until after the convention."

"Okay, but this will be good P.R. for both our department and the FBI. And Lord knows we could both use some good publicity. I know you've got to be busy. Call me later, when you have time to fill me in on the details."

When Bill hung up, Melissa walked into his office. He thought that she was probably watching his phone line, and waited until the light went out on the phone in the outer office to walk in. He appreciated her thoughtfulness – another sign of how good a job she was doing. She handed him the list of equipment everyone had said they needed for the Dallas trip. Don wanted a Lincoln Electric 185 Amp Outback Stick Welder, with a rack that included wheels. He also listed a specific model of Robovent. Arnie wanted a certain model drill, a socket set, insulated pliers, various screwdrivers and wrenches, a new carrying cart, and a circuit tester. Steve Jennings needed a new wire cutter, both Phillips and flathead screw drivers, and another set of pliers. At the bottom of the list Melissa had added the extension cord requirement, including the amperage the cord needed to be able to handle. There was a note attached from a second headquarters NES Team – "We'll have the same protective gear available you wore in Chicago."

Melissa saw Bill had finished scanning the list, so she asked, "Tell me what you need for a truck, and what the problem was with the van we used this morning. If that was an issue, we need to get something else in place right away."

Bill explained, "We had problems getting the bomb from Arnie's cart, which was about thirty inches higher than the dock, down to the level of the cradle in the van. The problem was that the van's floor was lower than the dock level, which meant we had to lower the bomb off the dock, and then raise it back up to get it on the cradle. We barely had enough people to keep from dropping the bomb. That was a pretty heavy load, and very unwieldy, and so we need to be able to move it from the cart into a cradle at that same height. That means we need to get the height of the loading dock at the Omni, find a truck that matches that height, and build a cradle in that truck approximately the same height as Arnie's cart. We want to be able to step straight from the dock into the back of the truck. If we can keep the bomb at or close to the same level when we are moving it, things will be tremendously easier."

"Okay, boss, I'm on it."

"And Melissa, thanks for coming in on a Sunday morning. You didn't have to be here, but I appreciate both you and Cindy going above and beyond the call of duty. On your way out, please ask Cindy to get me the Director on the phone. It's an hour later in D.C., and I imagine he's already in the office."

A minute later Bill's phone buzzed, again. "Mr. Director? Bill Peterson. We got our bomb disarmed, and NEST has it. We think we got in and out without anyone noticing, so our trap for Mohammed may still be good. Anything new on our interrogator from the Secretary of State's Office?"

"They are flying someone to Chicago this morning to meet with Abdul whatever his name is. I'm not really sure the interrogator is really from State, or is in the CIA, but they are supposedly sending their best person. Do you think you need to be there, to get Abdul to talk?"

"Not a bad idea, Sir. I can at least introduce the interrogator. They probably don't want me around during the questioning, but I can get the process started. I think Abdul will talk to anybody if it will help him save his skin."

The Director said, "He may end up getting sent to Guantanamo. It depends on how State wants to handle this. Personally, I'd like to charge him with everything under the sun, and put him on trial right there in Chicago, along with all of his team. But if he is cooperating, State may feel differently. Once politics get involved, normal procedures go out the window, and sometimes our prosecution plans get shut down. So, we'll see how we end up handling this. Good job with the bomb. Now get the one in Dallas disarmed, too, so that I can sleep a little better." Once again, the Director hung up before Bill could say another word.

Next, Bill tried to call Randy Marshall in Dallas, but he wasn't in the office, and Bill didn't think the call was important enough to get it transferred to Randy's cell. Bill left a message saying that the Chicago bomb had been successfully defused, and that the team would be arriving at Love Field's Signature Flight Support FBO at around noon on Monday.

By now it was late enough on Sunday morning that most people would be stirring, so Bill called Julie in Waco. "Hi, sweetheart. We got it done, with no major problems. We're all headed to Dallas on Monday. How are things in Waco?

"Mom says she'll put up with you for a few days, if she has to. I think she's kidding, but I'm not sure. Have you done anything lately to make her mad? "

Bill laughed. "Not that I know of. Maybe moving you to Chicago. I miss you, and can't wait to get to see you. Tell your Mom I'll take both of you out to the Magnolia Café for dinner, and maybe we'll run into Chip or Joanna."

Julie said, "Mom would probably go for that. I'll tell her, so she'll have something to look forward to when you get here. I love you, too. See you on Tuesday. Now go get some sleep."

Bill took her advice, and headed home. If he could get four hours in bed before the Secretary of State's interrogator got to MCC, Bill knew he would be a lot sharper and ready for whatever Abdul might try. It had been a long night, but the adrenaline rush was wearing off, and Bill knew he needed to crash for at least a few hours.

Chapter 27

Monday, June 1st

When Bill got to Midway, he found that the Signature FBO was a madhouse. Apparently, a lot of people liked to fly places on Monday mornings. He finally found the FBI jet, a Learjet 45 XR, configured with seats for eight people. Melissa was there, supervising the loading of their equipment, and checking things against a list she had on a clipboard.

Bill walked up to her, and she turned to acknowledge him when she saw him approaching. "All the gear is here, Bill, and now all we need are the rest of the passengers and their luggage."

"Can this plane handle luggage for five people, plus all the gear we are taking?"

Melissa nodded. "I asked, and the pilots tell me that is not a problem. We couldn't have taken one of the water heaters with us, so I'm glad we're getting that in Dallas. And, by the way, I'm planning on going with you."

"No, Melissa, you're not. I would love to have you along, to help make sure everything is working according to plan, but you being here, running the office while I'm gone, is more important."

Melissa shrugged. "Well, it was worth a try." One of the FBO staff people came up and took Bill's suitcase, and took it around to the far side of the plane to load it into the fuselage.

Bill said, "Who else is already here?"

"Steve Jennings and Don Czerwinski. They are in the lounge in the hanger. We're waiting on Rollings and Razolli." Bill walked into the hanger, but before he could get to the lounge James Rollings and Arnie Razolli walked up.

Bill said, "Okay, looks like everybody is here, and on time. I was just headed for the lounge. If you guys want a restroom break or a cup of coffee before we get out of here, now is the time. Give your suitcases to the guy out by the plane, and come on back into the lounge." James and Arnie nodded, and headed out to the plane. Bill found the lounge, and poured himself a cup of coffee. There were doughnuts and other pastries on a tray by the coffee urn, but Bill passed on those. Arnie came back in, picked up a doughnut, and took a bite.

"Wow! Krispy Kreme! These Signature people know how to treat their customers!" Everyone else in the lounge laughed.

The rest of the team stood up, and gathered around Bill. He said, "Take a piss break now, if you haven't already. I don't know how good the facilities will be on the plane. And it's about two hours to Dallas. After that, everybody on the plane. Your gear has already been loaded. We're ready to hit the friendly skies."

Ten minutes later a ground crewman shut the door to the plane, and the engines were started. A few minutes later they were in the air. Things were a little quiet on the plane, as everyone contemplated what they were trying to accomplish. They had gotten a little lucky with the first bomb, thanks to Arnie's sharp eyes. Could they pull off a second miracle? Everyone swallowed, and it wasn't just to relieve the pressure on their ears.

Two hours later, as they were landing at Love Field, they approached the airport from the south, and flew almost directly between the Reunion Tower and the Kay Bailey Hutchinson Convention Center. The Omni Hotel was located right between those two structures. The team got a bird's eye view of where they were going, even if was for just a few seconds. Steve Jennings tried to take some pictures out of the window of the plane where he was sitting, using the camera on his cell phone, but he didn't have time to check to see how good those pictures were as he was taking them. Three minutes later they were on the ground.

Randy Marshall met their plane. He had brought another eight-passenger van, so there was room for the entire team, their gear, and all their luggage. As he was climbing down the stairs from the plane, Bill spotted Randy waiting by the hanger.

"Hey, Randy. Nice of you to come out here and meet us. Everything ready to go for tonight?"

Randy shook his head. "We've got some issues to discuss. We're meeting the Omni's engineer for lunch, and we'll figure out how to do this. This won't be as easy as your Chicago B&E."

Bill laughed at Randy's reference to a burglary. "Okay, where are we going for lunch?"

Randy answered, "Actually, back to the Federal Building. We needed some privacy for what we need to talk about, so I'm having Texas barbeque catered in for lunch. In Texas, you'll find great barbeque and Mexican food. I suggest Mexican for dinner, if everyone is not too full from lunch. Both are different from what you find up north, but I think your bunch will like it. Our office here is just north of Love Field, so this will be a short trip. I'd rather wait and explain everything when everybody is sitting down, paying attention, and can hear what we have to say."

Ten minutes later they pulled into the parking garage at the Federal Building on Justice Way. Everyone was led to a first-floor conference room, where a buffet lunch was already set out and waiting. The servers had been dismissed, with orders to come back and clean up after 2:00 in the afternoon. That would give Randy and the team time to talk.

Also waiting for them were Ricky English and Joan Samuelson from the Omni. After everyone filled their plates and sat down, Randy introduced the guests from the hotel. "Ricky is the hotel manager, and Joan is the Chief Engineer. Both these two know about the bomb, and they are here to help us figure out how to get in and out of the hotel as surreptitiously as possible. Joan has a slide show and even a video to show you that explains the problems, and her suggested solutions. Feel free to ask questions, but it might be better to wait until after she finishes her presentation. Joan, the floor is yours."

Joan asked that the lights be dimmed as she turned on the projector hooked up to her laptop. "Go ahead and eat. Although what I have to say may ruin your appetite. The bomb is located in a storage area under one of our ballrooms, in the section of the hotel that connects the sleeping rooms with the convention center. We have a Skybridge walkway running between the hotel and the convention center, and our ballroom area is beneath that Skybridge, with storage on the first floor, and ballrooms on the second and third floors. This first slide is a diagram of the entire site, to give you the big picture. Any questions on this?"

No one said anything, so she continued. She changed the slide to show a picture of the front of the hotel and the loading dock. "Both the hotel and our ballroom area share one loading dock area, which is located just around the corner from our main hotel entrance. So, anyone coming or going from the hotel entrance, or even standing outside smoking a cigarette, can see what is happening at that loading dock. A team coming into the loading dock, even at one or two in the morning, faces too big a chance of being seen and an alarm being raised. The same problem would apply if the team tried to approach the area by coming in through the Skybridge from the convention center. There are windows down the length of the Skybridge, and it is lit up and visible from about fifty restaurants and bars in what we call our Arts District. If the team came in through the Skybridge, especially in your protective gear, a picture of you would probably be on the front page of the Dallas

Morning News before you even got out of the building.

The only possible solution I see is to hide the team in the building before things get too quiet in the evening. You can don your protective gear in the room we put you in, and then move from there to the room holding the bomb. Like what you did in Chicago, we have cameras monitoring the hallways, stairs, and elevators, so we will be able to tell you when it is safe to move.

Coming out with the bomb, once it is disarmed, is a different matter. I don't see any way out of the building other than using that loading dock. So, I'm suggesting we don't try and hide that operation. Once you disarm the bomb, you leave it in place in our storeroom for the rest of the night. Later Tuesday morning, a plumbing truck will show up at our dock, unload a dummy water heater shell, take it to that storeroom, and remove the bomb. That may expose a few more people to a little radioactivity, but from the dosimeter results I saw from your Chicago experience, the danger there is minimal. The team will go back into hiding and change back into civilian clothing. The

NES Team will collect your exposed protective gear and clothing, and take that out inside lead lined bags. You'll need to wait until there are enough people around that you can slip out of the hotel without being noticed. Then you can go for your firehose showers. I'm open to suggestions, but I don't see any other way to get the team in and out of the hotel without alarms being raised, especially if we still want to have a water heater in place to try and lure in our terrorist during the convention. Okay, the floor is open for suggestions and questions."

Bill took a sip of his sweet iced tea, and stood up. "I like your idea of hiding in the hotel until we can go after the bomb, but I don't like the idea of sitting around after we get it disarmed. Leaving the bomb there until later Tuesday morning is fine, but we need to get the team out of there and cleaned up. Plus, we'll have to set something up with a fake plumber to take in the dummy heater and bring out the bomb. Maybe people on the NES Team can handle that. Randy, Melissa Anderson was supposed to have contacted you about the truck that was

321

needed to load the bomb. Do you have that vehicle ready?"

Randy had a mouthful of brisket, but he nodded yes.

Bill continued. "My suggestion would be to change back into civilian clothing, and then maybe split up, so it doesn't look like we're a group of five. A couple of guys could just go out through the hotel lobby. That's not too unusual, even at 5:00 in the morning. The rest of us could go down the Skybridge to the convention center, and leave through one of their exits. We might be noticed, but probably not connected to any activity at the hotel. We could meet up once we were all outside, and head somewhere for our showers. What do the rest of you think?"

Randy stood up. "I agree with Bill. I don't like the idea of the team sitting around after being exposed to radiation, even if the chances of a big dose are very small. We need to get them cleaned up as soon as possible. Plus, that will be easier to do while it is still dark. Joan, I like your ideas on getting the team in place, and the bomb back out of the building, but I think we need to go with Bill's team extraction plan.

Joan looked at her boss, Ricky English, and nodded. He nodded back, and the issue was settled.

"Okay," Joan said. "Now I want to show you a video of the inside of our storage area in the hotel. I want you to be able to visualize where you will be staging, and which way you'll have to go to get to the water heater storeroom." She started the video. "This is the second floor of the ballroom area. This is our tech area, where we have setups to control audio/visual presentations in our ballrooms. There is a back-storage room off the tech area that, as of right now, is not being used. I think that empty room would be perfect for your staging area. We still have to figure out a way to get the protective gear down to that room without anyone getting suspicious, and how to sneak the team down there, too. From the tech area you would be moving south, down this hallway, to this elevator, and then down one floor to our storage area. Then you would go back north three doors, and the room you want will be on your right. I'll give someone a passkey so that you can access the elevator and the storeroom door.

Once you're done in the storeroom, you return the same way to the tech room to change clothes. Leaving the tech room, two people will go south to the stairway next to the elevator, and go back down to the first floor. The doorway at the bottom of that stairway opens into the main hotel lobby. The other three guys will go to the same south stairway, but go up the stairs instead of down. Once you reach the third floor, you'll be right by the Skybridge, and can head over towards the convention center. We'll have to somehow get the NES Team back to the tech room to clean up everything, but we'll figure that out later. Randy, can you contact the NES Team leader, and have him meet me in my office at 2:00? I'd like to show him what we need, and where his team will be operating. Bill, is there anyone on your team that you want to send on that tour? Or, would you like to go?"

Bill spoke up first. "Steve Jennings is your equivalent from the Hyatt in Chicago. I think he would be the best person to tour your facility from our team. Steve, can you meet Joan at the Omni at 2:00? And that reminds me. Where are we staying? We all need to check into our rooms, and Steve needs to do it quickly if he is going to be back at the Omni in a couple of hours."

Randy said, "I'll have the van driver take all of you to your hotel as soon as you finish lunch. We have you staying at the Crowne Plaza, just a few blocks north of the Omni. I'll contact our NES Team leader, Bill Burke, and have him report to Joan at 2:00 this afternoon. They'll not be happy about leaving the bomb in place, even for a few hours, but I agree with everyone else that bringing it out through the loading dock during normal hours is probably the best plan. I'll give Bill that bit of bad news. Anyone else have anything we need to discuss? Okay, I'll see all of you at dinner. Meeting adjourned."

The team was driven to the Crowne Plaza, and everyone went through the check-in line. Bill gathered the team, and told them. "I know it won't be easy, but try and get some rest this afternoon. I need all of you to be sharp tonight. We'll meet back down here in the lobby at 6:00. Randy is going to take all of us to dinner, and then we'll go to the Omni. So, bring your clothes you plan to

325

wear tomorrow down with you. That's why we told all of you to bring an extra backpack. Plus, we'll look more like hotel guests at the Omni if we are carrying clothes when we go through that place later this evening."

Everyone headed for their rooms to unpack. Bill had some calls to return. Steve quickly unpacked, and headed back downstairs. He asked the concierge behind the desk in the lobby, "I have a meeting at the Omni. Is that walkable? Or do I need a taxi?"

"Sir, it is only about five or six blocks, but it is hot outside. I suggest a taxi, or Uber, this afternoon."

"Thanks. Are there taxis out front?"

"Yes, sir. Just tell the doorman you need a taxi, and he'll whistle for the first in line."

Ten minutes later, Steve was in the Omni, and asking for Joan Samuelson. "Please tell her Steve Jennings is here to see her."

A minute later Joan came from a back office, smiled at Steve, and led him back to her office. "Thanks for coming on over. We have a lot of details to work through."

Steve looked around, noticing that her office was about twice the size of his in

Chicago. "Nice office. Bigger than mine. And that's a beautiful picture. Your daughter?"

"Yep. My daughter, Liz. She just graduated from UT Austin, with a Petroleum Engineering degree, and will be working in Houston, making more with her starting salary than I do here at the hotel, even after being here for ten years."

"You've been here that long?" Steve said. "That's a long time to be in one place, in our profession."

Joan smiled. "I moved to Dallas ten years ago, after I got divorced. Liz was here with me, during her high school years, but its been just me for the last four years. It was awkward at Liz's graduation, because my ex showed up, too, and I had to pretend to be nice to him for that entire weekend.

Steve laughed. "I just went through the same thing. I've been divorced for fifteen years, but my daughter got married up in Michigan a couple of weeks ago, and of course she wanted her mom to be at the wedding, too. So, my ex and I had to be civil to each other, as difficult as that was. Maybe when this is all over, we can have dinner and compare war stories."

Joan said, "Well, maybe if you're still around. Just because you successfully disarmed one bomb doesn't guarantee success on ours."

"Thanks a lot for that vote of confidence." They both laughed.

Bill Burke, the NES Team leader, was led into Joan's office and everyone introduced themselves. Joan told them, "We've got cameras set up throughout the storage area, including all the access points, and the FBI has had a team in place in our parking garage since this morning, monitoring those cameras. We have enough walkie-talkies and blue tooth earpieces for the NES Team and the disarmament team, so that everyone can hear what the monitoring team is saying. I'm going to give both of you passkeys that will let you in anywhere in the building. If possible, I would like those back when this operation is over, even if we have to clean them if they end up being contaminated. I have to report all lost passkeys, so it would be a lot easier if they could be cleaned and returned.

Bill, the plan is for you to lead your team to the tech room late this afternoon, as if you are setting up for a presentation tomorrow. We see people doing that all the time. Your team can easily slip from the tech room to the back-storage room, and set out all the protection gear for our disarmament team. I suggest you, or some member of your team, stay there to help the team get their gear in place when they arrive. The rest of your team will leave after getting the gear in place, just as they would if they were setting up for a presentation.

Steve, we'll have your Bill – that may end up being confusing – and the rest of your team here later this evening, after dinner. As the monitoring team gives an all clear, we'll have team members slip into the stairway next to my office, and head down to the tech area. I'm going to take both of you down that way now, so you'll know the way. I don't know if it would be better for your entire team to head down at one time, or do it a couple of people at a time. I'll leave that up to Bill Peterson. It might be better if you all went at once, because that way, Steve, you could serve as the guide as to which way to go."

Chapter 28

There was a second of blinding light, searing pain, and then everything went black. Bill could feel his soul soaring up the air, and giving him a birds-eye view of the scene from about a half-mile up in the air. There was nothing but a big hole where the Omni and the convention center once stood. The Reunion Tower had been knocked on its side, and cracked into several pieces. It was dark out, but fires burning from the blast lit the scene like it was midday. Cars and semis were turned over and thrown into a pile on both Interstates 35 and 30, and a new vehicle gas tank cooked off every few seconds. Bill could hear a ringing sound in his ears, but then it hit him that he shouldn't have any ears left. Then he realized it really was a ringing sound, and coming from his bedside phone. "Sir, this is your 5:30 PM wakeup call, as requested." Bill had been having a nightmare, and this was one he didn't want to repeat.

Fifteen minutes later he was in the lobby, freshly showered, and carrying a backpack.

The rest of the team showed up in the next few minutes, and they went outside to wait for Randy and his van. Dinner was pretty subdued. The Mexican food was some of the best they had ever eaten, but they were too keyed up to really enjoy it. Bill had another fleeting thought – was a lot of greasy Mexican food the best thing to eat, if they were all going to be locked in a small room together for the next several hours?

Bill reminded the team that he had promised them a steak dinner on Tuesday if everything went well. By 8:30, they were hiding in their tech room at the Omni, waiting on the place to get quiet. Most of the hotel staff was gone by 10:00, apart from a few late-night baristas and room service waiters. The hotel restaurants closed, and other than a few hotel guests serious about their drinking, the entire place seemed to be deserted. The team was lucky that there were no banquets or late-night meetings being held in the two hotel ballrooms, so that section of the hotel got eerily quiet.

By 11:00 the team was going stir crazy, so Bill told them to suit up. The remaining NES Team member helped everyone get their gear on, and they checked out the equipment that Randy had provided. They seemed to have all the stuff they needed, so they waited for clearance to go. Finally, at midnight, the camera monitoring team reported that all was clear. Quietly, they crept out of their hiding hole, walked to the elevator, and headed for the first floor. Steve led the way, having been shown where to go by Joan Samuelson. Once in the storeroom with the bomb, everyone took their assigned place. Bill locked the door behind them. One last check was made with the monitors, who reported everything was still quiet. Arnie pulled out his portable drill and socket wrench, and started removing bolts.

Steve told Don, "Don't wait for us to get the top off. Go ahead and start cutting your square around the LED display. That will save us a few minutes, while Arnie and I work on the top section." Don fired up his portable welder, and James Rollings held the hose, sucking up the fumes coming from the cut. Two minutes later the top was off the water heater, and Steve could start cutting wires from the batteries. Everyone breathed a sigh of relief when the last wire was cut in the top section of the heater.

But when Steve removed the first battery box, Don yelled, "Wait! Something just started a timer on the LED display. The thing is counting down from two minutes!"

Steve asked him. "Can you finish your square and get it pulled away from the heater before the counter finishes?"

Don said, "I don't think so!"

Steve told James Rollings, "Give me a hand, here." Don had the top three sides of the cut completed, an inverted "U." Steve used a pair of pliers to pry the edge of the cut away from the rest of the heater, and then he and James grabbed the hot edge of the cut piece and pulled it downward, exposing the hole into the heater. Both were wearing gloves, but the hot metal still burned their fingers through their glove tips.

Don said, "The timer is down to thirty seconds!" The LED display was pulled away from the bomb when the metal piece was pulled down, but it was still attached to the detonators. Steve took his wire cutters and started cutting the wires between the LED box and the detonator packs of plastic explosives. Fifteen seconds later that was done, and then he cut the wires leading from the timer back to the top of the water heater. The timer stopped with eight seconds still showing.

Everybody looked at each other, wondering what they had just done. Steve said, "Either they added a new booby trap to this bomb, or somehow we failed to set it off on the other one. Once again, we got lucky. If Don hadn't already almost finished his cut around the LED box, we would have been goners. We need to be extra careful with the rest of this, just to make sure there aren't any more surprises." He started pulling the packets of plastic explosives out of the cavity in the center of the heater. "I'm going to go ahead and finish this area, before we go back to the top."

He did it slowly, but five minutes later the explosives were in Rollings' backpack. He moved back to the top of the water heater, and finished pulling the batteries – but checking to make sure there were no additional tripwires attached. Don cut the top pressure plate away from the heater's interior, and Steve pulled out those detonator packs, too. Thirty minutes later they were done. Bill looked at his watch. He was sure they had been in that storeroom for at least three hours, but was surprised to find that it was only 1:15 in the morning. They had been in the room for only a little over an hour. They closed the openings in the bomb, packed up all their equipment, got clearance from the camera monitors, and headed back to the tech room. By 1:30 they had again taken off all of their protective gear, were back to what they were originally wearing, and were ready to head out. Bill told them, "Good job, everyone. I knew we had a great team, and you proved it again tonight. Steve, James, how are your hands?"

Steve answered, "The burns are only minor – probably light second degree, or maybe like a bad sunburn. We'll be okay with a little burn ointment."

Don pulled a tube out of his backpack. "Every welder carries burn ointment. Burns are a part of the job."

Bill said, "I've changed my mind on how we exfiltrate. I think it is still early enough we could all leave together, out the front of the hotel, like we were all headed to a bar for

335

one last round. Let's hit the road." Bill called Randy, who was with the NES Team leader, and they promised to have the van out in front of the hotel by the time the team could get out the door. Five minutes later they were headed for their pressure wash showers.

The City of Dallas was building a new park that was going to run the length of the Trinity River, running almost parallel to Interstate 35E as the highway, and the river, circled around the west side of downtown. Randy Marshall had gotten the same deal Bill had gotten in Chicago. The Dallas police had closed off a section of the park that was not yet open to the public, so that the NES Team could set up in privacy.   The bomb disarmament team got one surprise when they got to the park – Joan Samuelson was waiting with the NES Team. Bill filled her in, along with Randy and Bill Burke, as the rest of the team took their showers and got dressed. As the team leader, Bill Peterson felt that it was important that he go last, to show that the rest of the team counted for something. But before long he was getting blasted by the pressure washer, too.

Randy Marshall said, "Great job, guys. Bill told me how cool you all acted under pressure. And I don't mean from the hose." This got a laugh. "Steve, once again, thank you for saving our city. We owe you a big one."

Steve said, "It took all of us, acting together. We couldn't have done it without each other."

Bill Burke said, "We're all set to switch out the water heaters in the morning, and your bomb will be gone. We'll take care of all the gear in that tech room, and sterilize that room, too. I want to thank all of you from keeping us from having to do our main job — clean up after a nuclear explosion."

Bill Peterson said, "Well, it was close. We did have eight seconds left on that timer."

Randy Marshall said, "Okay, everybody back in the van. We'll take you back to the hotel. I'm sure you all want another shower to get that disinfectant small off of you. I'll notify everybody necessary that the bomb has been disarmed. You can all get some sleep, and we'll debrief all of you later this morning. I'll have the van pick you up around 10:00 in front of the hotel."

Joan Samuelson spoke up. "I've got some more questions for Steve, so I'm taking him with me. I'll make sure he's at the hotel in the morning. Steve looked at Bill Peterson, who just shrugged. Steve looked at Joan, and nodded. They headed for her car.

When they were on the road, Steve asked, "Where are we going? Back to the Omni?"

"My place. You need a shower."

"Yes, I do."

"And my shower is big enough for two, if the two are willing to get close."

"I think we can handle that."

Chapter 29

Tuesday, June 2nd

Bill called Julie on Tuesday morning, just to assure her that all was well, but that he wouldn't make it to Waco until Wednesday. Tuesday was full of debriefings for all the team members, along with official warnings to forget everything they had seen and heard. Both Don Czerwinski and Arnie Razolli were told to complete invoices for their time, and they gleefully set to working on that paperwork, knowing that this project was going to pay for quite a summer vacation for their families. Don called his wife, and asked, "When do the kids get out of school?"

"End of next week."

"You ready for that trip to Disney World you've always wanted? Plan on leaving a day or two after they get out of school. We're going for a whole week!"

Randy Marshall called Bill Tuesday morning, to tell Bill that the water heater switch at the Omni had gone well, and that the bomb was finally gone. "And tell Melissa Anderson that if she ever wants a transfer to Texas, for her to call me. We owe her one." Bill promised to let her know.

Tuesday night Bill took the whole team to Ruth's Chris Steakhouse, just north of downtown on Cedar Springs Road. The bill came out to about $125 per person, but Bill didn't care. He put it on his government American Express Card. He wondered if the Director was going to get a letter about Bill's profligate spending, like the letter Bill had received about Chet Kingsley, and that the Director might have a coronary when he saw how much Bill had spent over the last week. And that reminded Bill that he needed to go see Chet when Bill got back to Chicago. They had a lot to discuss.

Wednesday morning Bill rented a car, and drove to Waco. The rest of the team flew home on the FBI's Learjet. Except for Steve Jennings. He called his boss, Lisa Brooks, at the Hyatt, and told her he was stressed out from his experiences, and needed a few days to unwind. He told her he would be back in the office on Monday. He hung up his cell phone, turned back to Joan, and said, "Now, where were we?"

Melissa Anderson met the team at Signature Flight at Chicago's Midway Airport, and gave them another new full set of tools and gear - along with checks for Don and Arnie. She reminded them, one more time, that they couldn't talk about their experience with anyone, at least until the FBI released the news about the bombs. And she told them that may never happen, and they would have to take this secret to their graves. They headed home, and she gave James Rollings a ride back to the FBI office in the Federal Building. Along the way, while they were stopped at a red light, he asked her, "You got dinner plans for tonight?"

She looked over at him. "Nope."

"Want to go grab some Italian? I'm tired of Texas food, and need some Chicago soul cooking."

Melissa laughed. "Sure. Your fingers okay? I heard about what you and Steve did to get into the bomb with the timer running down."

"Well, I'm not ready to do pushups, but I can hold a fork. Pick you up at 7:00?"

"Sounds great."

They didn't say another word as they finished the drive, and pulled into the parking garage.

Chapter 30

Monday, June 8th

The Director called Bill Peterson at 8:00 Chicago time Monday morning. "Just to fill you in, we got a lot from Abdul from Afghanistan. Since then, the CIA has been tracking down leads, and we now know that Iran was definitely involved on the smuggling end. That doesn't rule out the DPRK, because Abdul tells us that when they asked questions about how the bomb was manufactured, the Iranians couldn't tell them much – so maybe the Iranians didn't make the bombs, but somehow got them from North Korea. We're following up on that lead, too. That's all I can say, but what you did may lead to some major changes in the world, and you can be proud.

What I'm really calling about is Chet Kingsley. You know we agreed to let him stay on as an agent, but he'll not be allowed to keep his ASAC position. It's probably a good idea for him to leave Chicago, so that he's not working along side people he used to supervise. I'm emailing you a list of vacant agent slots around the country. Tell him we'll pay all moving expenses, but he is going to have to move. Let me know what he decides. Have you thought about his replacement?

"Sir, Melissa Anderson has been doing a great job. She is detail oriented, and I need somebody like that to keep me focused when I get too enamored with the 'big picture." I would like to announce her promotion as soon as you can get that approved."

"Consider it done. You can go ahead and tell her. But remember to email me back on where Chet wants to go. He has been a good career agent, so I want to give him a second chance."

Bill called up his email, printed off the list of available vacancies, and told Cindy he was heading over to see Chet. She called the rehab facility, to make sure they knew Bill was coming, and that it was official business, and not just a friend visiting a friend.

Thirty minutes later Bill pulled into Gateway. He went through the usual check-in procedure, and was led to a private room, where Chet was waiting.

"Chet, you look 100% better than you did the last time I was here."

"I feel 100% better. They are going to let me out of here before too long, and I need to know what I'll be doing."

"That's why I'm here," Bill said. He pulled out his list. The Director called me this morning, wanting to talk about you. He cares about you, and wants you to have a fresh start – but it will have to be somewhere else. You knew you wouldn't be getting your old job back, and he feels, and I agree, that it would not be a good idea for you to be working with the agents that you used to supervise. Look over this list, and tell me what interests you."

Chet skimmed it quickly. "Glenwood Springs, Colorado. A small town, so it will be a small FBI unit, probably just two or three agents. I can get more hands-on in a place like that, and handle lots of different types of cases, compared to what I would be assigned to do in a big office. Plus, my wife and I love to ski, and that is close to the mountains. And Glenwood has the biggest damn natural swimming pool you've ever seen – and you can swim in it year-round. If you can get me Glenwood, I would be forever grateful."

"The Director told me to tell you that you could have anything on the list, and that the FBI would be paying full moving expenses. So, Glenwood Springs it is. Let me know when you're going to get out of here, so that we can start the moving paperwork." They shook hands, and Bill left, feeling like he had done his good deed for the day.

Chapter 31

Monday, June 15th

The 35-foot Bertram crept slowly into the Port Hope Marina. Pete Hanson reversed the engines, stopping the boat just as it kissed the edge of the dock. He shut everything down, satisfied that another run had gone smoothly. He looked up and down the dock, but only saw a couple of fishermen jigging their lines up and down, sitting on an otherwise empty dock a couple of spaces down the line from Pete's boat. This time Pete had gone out with one customer, but come back with two. He nodded to the two men, telling them that it was okay to leave the cabin of the boat.

They had apparently called ahead to their ride, because a minivan was coming down the hill toward the docks. It stopped at the empty parking space next to Pete's boat, as if awaiting Pete's customers. But when the two customers stepped out on the dock, the doors to the minivan opened, and four guys in FBI vests climbed out, all holding pistols. Pete heard a sound from the other end of the dock, and found that the two guys that had been fishing were also pointing pistols at Pete and the two other guys on his boat. "Pete Hanson? You're under arrest for smuggling. And you two are also under arrest. You, for aiding and abetting an illegal entry into the United States. And you, for attempting to illegally enter the United States. You may all be charged with additional crimes at a later time, so you should be warned that anything you say may be used against you in a court of law. And if you are who we think you are, Kitab al-Hawi, you are on our list of the ten most wanted terrorists from Iran. I'm sure you came to America just to surrender to us. Sam, cuff all three of them and put them in the van." Ten minutes later the van was on its way back to Detroit, with the prisoners cuffed and shackled to hooks in the floor of the van. A call was made to the Detroit SAC, and after he got the news on the arrests, he called Bill Peterson.

"Bill? Charlie Rogers over in Detroit. Your tip on Pete Hanson paid off big time. We caught him trying to smuggle in a terrorist named Kitab al-Hawi, a really big fish. Andy Renner, from your office, was in on the bust, and I'll make sure the Director knows what Andy did to help us get onto Hanson. Just wanted to say thanks for your help on this one. Goes to show what we can do when we work together on a case. So, thanks, again. Call me if we can do anything for Chicago."

Charlie's comment about working together had put a devilish thought into Bill's mind, and he decided that he had built up enough good will with the Director that he could get away with it. Bill called Arnie Razolli. "Arnie? This is Bill Peterson. And before you have a heart attack, I'm not asking you to volunteer for anything, at least this time around. But I do need something from you. Are you installing any Rheem water heaters any time soon, or have you installed one in the last few days? I'm looking for a Rheem cardboard box, not the water heater itself. Do you have access to an empty Rheem box?"

Arnie was quiet for a moment. "I thought you were calling about another bomb. I was about to tell you to find somebody else – I've had enough excitement over the last few weeks to last me a lifetime. But a box I can do. I've actually got a Rheem in my truck, to be delivered tomorrow. It is not as big as the ones we worked on – does that matter?"

Bill said, "Nope. All I'm looking for is a slice out of that box, a square from one side of the box, showing the Rheem logo. Can you save me a piece of the box after you install your heater?"

"No problem. I can have the box for you tomorrow evening. Want me to bring it by your office?"

"No, I'll come by your shop and pick it up. Maybe on Wednesday morning? And thanks again, Arnie, for what you did. You helped to save a couple of America's finest cities, and you can be proud of the work you did."

"Okay, I'll leave it here tomorrow evening, and you can pick it up on Wednesday. And thanks for the kind words."

Chapter 32

Wednesday, June 17th

Bill picked up the piece of cardboard that simply said, "Rheem," from Arnie's plumbing shop, and headed straight for the nearest Michaels Store. At the rear of the store was a custom framing shop. "Yes, sir, may I help you?"

"I need this piece of cardboard framed, with a glass top, and then the entire thing packaged up and mailed to a co-worker. Can your shop handle that?"

The clerk didn't say anything about the strange request for framing. Bill was sure she had seen things a lot weirder than his piece of cardboard come across that counter. "Yes, sir. Just pick out a color and size you want for the frame, and give us the address where you want the package mailed. One point, since you asked for glass. We package our stuff well, to try and protect the glass, but we can't guarantee the glass won't crack while in the mail stream."

Bill nodded his acceptance, picked out a frame, and gave them the address for mailing the package. "I want it sent to Angela Robertson, Special Agent in Charge, FBI Office, 1250 Poydras Street, New Orleans, Louisiana, 70113." Bill had to spell Poydras for the clerk at the counter, but five minutes later he had paid for the framing and the mailing, and he was on his way back to his office. He doubted that he would ever hear anything from Angela about getting the package, but he was sure that she would get the message.

Chapter 33

Thursday, July 23rd

This election cycle it was the Republican's turn to hold the first nominating convention, and their festivities had been going full swing all week in Chicago. Tonight was the culmination, with the nominee giving his acceptance speech, and the "official" nomination of the nominee's hand-picked vice-presidential choice. The McCormick Place Convention Center was rocking, but things were pretty quiet across the street at the Hyatt.

It was close to 10:00 PM when the door swung open to the storeroom in the basement of the Hyatt. The light was turned on, and the visitor quickly headed for the three water heaters. Behind him, Mohammed heard, "Looking for this?" When he turned, Agent James Rollings was there, holding the remote that had been removed from the bomb – and also holding a pistol on Mohammed. Two other agents were blocking the door. "Abriz Mohammed, you are under arrest for attempting to use a weapon of mass destruction against the United States of America." And the Chicago domestic terrorism cell was completely out of business.

Chapter 34

Friday, July 24th

When it was 10:00 PM in Chicago, it was already 2:00 in the afternoon of the next day in Pyongyang, North Korea. General Shin Tse Kue had been a chess prodigy in his youth – known for being able to see at least three plays ahead on the game board. That same talent had served him well in the military as he rose through the ranks of the People's Army. General Shin had been a pilot in his younger days, and his rank allowed him the privilege of staying current in whatever fighters the North Korean military had in their arsenal. This afternoon he had scheduled a refresher flight in a Mig-29 Fulcrum, the most potent of the DPRK's Army-Air Force fighters. The fighter was awaiting him when he arrived at the base outside of Pyongyang.

This particular Mig was configured as a two-seater trainer, unusual for the Mig-29, so when General Shin walked out to the plane with a diminutive copilot no one paid any attention to the copilot, who was already wearing a helmet. The ground crewman assigned to the plane saluted the General, and the salute was returned. The crewman watched as the General assisted the copilot into the back seat of the plane, and helped the copilot to strap in. "Now, that is something you don't see every day," thought the crewman. "I thought the copilot was the one training the General on this aircraft." The General climbed the ladder to the front cockpit, started the engines, and closed the canopy.

He contacted the tower, who gave him immediate approval to taxi and take off. Other than the Supreme Leader, General Shin got priority wherever he went. If he wanted a jet fighter to play with, he got a jet fighter. Five minutes later he ran up the engines at the end of the runway, and then released the brakes. Twenty seconds later he was off the ground. He headed northeast, towards Chongjin and the border with China, and away from any possible difficulties that could arise if you got too close to the border with South Korea. He climbed to 6,000 feet, but then suddenly dove rapidly back toward the ground. "Mayday! Mayday! My plane has lost hydraulic pressure, and I've lost aileron and elevator control. We may be going down!"

"Understood, General. You know the emergency procedures. Eject if you must. We'll get a rescue helicopter headed your way."

But when the plane got down to around 1000 feet off the ground, the General started pulling out of the dive, and leveled off just above the rice fields he was flying over. He turned off his radio and IDF, the device that identifies individual planes on radar, and pulled a remote control out of the pocket of his flight suit. He pushed the button on the remote, and a large explosion occurred on the ground just ahead and to the west of his plane's location. He had timed it well, and it looked like his plane had gone down. He stayed low, underneath any possible radar coverage, turned to the east, and ten minutes later he was out over the Sea of Japan. He turned to the southeast, towards Ishikawa.

An hour later he was approaching Japan's coastline, when he had Japanese fighters suddenly appear on each side of his aircraft. He was contacted on the Military Air Distress (MAD) channel, also known as UHF Guard, at 243 MHz "North Korean Aircraft, please state your intentions."

"This is General Shin Tse Kue. I am defecting, and bringing Japan the gift of this aircraft. As you can see, the aircraft is unarmed. If you will direct me to the nearest military air base, I'll be happy to land wherever you desire."

"General Shin, please follow me to Yokota Air Force Base. What is your fuel status? "

"No problem on fuel. I know Yokota is the other side of Tokyo proper. Do you want me to fly around that city?"

"Yes, sir, please. We'll direct you south of Tokyo, and then back north to Yokota. When we approach Tokyo, we ask that you lower your landing gear, so that we know you don't have any untoward intentions."

General Shin said, "Will do. Just let me know what you want, and when you want it."

Thirty minutes later he was on the ground at Yokota. "Sir, a follow me truck will lead you away from our staging areas. You will be met by an armed guard. Please understand why we have to take these precautions."

"I understand, and will comply. I ask that you not shoot me or my copilot when we disembark from the plane."

"Our soldiers are well disciplined, sir. Just don't make any sudden moves."

Five minutes later General Shin shut down his fighter, opened the cockpit, and then turned to his copilot. "Well, dearest wife, we may have escaped Kim Jong-un's prison after all."

He helped her climb down from the plane, and then told her to take off her helmet. He saw the troops holding rifles on them visually relax when they saw that the copilot was an older woman. A captain walked up to the general, and saluted. "Sir, I am Captain Sato. I understand that you wish to defect?"

"Yes, and I have information vital to the interests of the United States. I need to talk to someone from the U.S. State Department, or the CIA, as soon as possible. Lives may be at stake, and this information needs to get back to the United States within the next few hours."

"Yes, sir. I'll see what I can do to set that up. Sir, is your copilot your wife?"

"That is correct, captain. If I had not brought her with me, she would have been tortured by Kim Jong-un. We are grateful for whatever you can do for us."

An hour later, Shin was meeting with a representative from the U.S. Embassy in Tokyo, telling them about the bombs that had been smuggled into the United States. Shin had no way of knowing that the FBI had already disarmed his bombs, but he suspected that something was amiss, because the first bomb had not gone off when expected in Chicago. By telling the United States about the bombs, Shin was hedging his bet – but also confirming that the bombs originated in North Korea.

The U.S. Embassy staffer, actually a CIA employee, told General Shin, "General, we already knew about the bombs, and they have been disarmed. Unless you have something else of equal importance to reveal, I don't see how you can be of any great service to the United States, and I'm not sure we will be willing to grant you the asylum you are requesting."

General Shin nearly panicked. "I can also give you Kim Jong-un's daily calendar for the next thirty days. I oversaw his personal security, so I had to know where he would be at all times. Would that be helpful?"

"Possibly. Give us the information, and we'll see what we can do with that, if anything. I'll get back to you on your request for asylum for you and your wife. I'm sure someone from the military will want to debrief you further, and if you are cooperative that will help your case."

Chapter 35

Wednesday, August 12th

Brady Worthington's capture in Dallas happened almost like the trap the FBI had set in Chicago for Mohammed, but Worthington did not go down without a fight. When he was confronted in the storeroom at the Omni, he tried to make a run for it. He slapped away the pistol of the agent closest to him, and took a swing at the agent standing in the door of the storeroom. An agent just outside the door stepped up and zapped Worthington with a stun gun, and that finally put him down. The terrorists that had set the bombs were now all in custody. On Thursday, the FBI put out a press release.

August 13

The FBI is announcing the capture of Brady Worthington, one of the leaders of the group known as "Secede or Die," a right-wing extremist group headquartered in Texas. The FBI also captured Abriz

Mohammed in Chicago, the leader of a domestic terrorist ring in that city. Both Worthington and Mohammed were instrumental in placing RDD explosive devices in Dallas and Chicago, with the intent of disrupting the Democratic and Republican National Conventions. The FBI discovered the plot, found the bombs, disarmed them, and removed them before any action could be taken by the named terrorist groups.

The FBI would like to thank Grant, Michigan Chief of Police John Bradley, the police departments of Chicago and Dallas, and various other individuals for their assistance in discovering the plot, finding the bombs, and helping to disarm and dispose of the bombs.

You can feel safe, knowing that all law enforcement agencies are putting their combined efforts into stopping terrorism, wherever and whenever terrorists may try and strike.

Bill Peterson saw the press release, and smiled. "Cindy, please see if you can get me Annie Jones at ABC7 on the phone."

His phone buzzed, and he picked up the receiver.

"Ms. Jones? This is Bill Peterson, with the FBI here in Chicago. We met, briefly, in the Federal Building parking garage a month or so back."

"I remember you, Agent Peterson. What can I do for you?"

"Actually, its what I'm going to do for you. Have you seen the press release the FBI put out about terrorist being captured, and bombs being disarmed in Chicago and Dallas?"

"No, but give me thirty seconds."

A minute later, Annie was back on the phone. "Okay, I'm reading the press release now."

Bill said, "I owe you after treating you so harshly in the parking garage. I'm going to give you three names. Steve Jennings is the Chief Engineer at the Hyatt next to the convention center. Don Czerwinski is a welder here in Chicago, and Arnie Razolli is a plumber, also working here in Chicago. You shouldn't have any trouble locating any of them. I suggest you take a camera crew and interview each of them about the part they played in helping to disarm the bomb here in Chicago, and the bomb in Dallas. You can tell them that I said it was now okay to talk. They may want to call me to verify that, but I'm giving them permission to open up to the press."

Annie was quiet for a few seconds. "And what do you want from me in return?"

"Just treat them fairly. They are civilians, not law enforcement officers. Each of them volunteered to assist us, and each of them had special skills that we needed. They helped save two of our finest cities, and they should be treated as heroes."

"Okay, Agent Peterson. Thanks for the tip. If this pans out, maybe we can say some nice things about the FBI, too."

Chapter 36

Friday, August 14th

Glenn Simpson, the Chicago Police Chief, called Bill at 6:00 AM. "I just heard your name on the morning news, so I thought I'd give you a call."

Bill groaned. "I guess this is payback for when I called you that Sunday morning?"

Glenn laughed. "Yep. But the lady on the news was interviewing three of the guys that worked with you to disarm the bombs, and they all said that you were the team leader. I'm thinking that now would be a good time to put you up for membership in the Union League, if you are interested in joining our little club."

"I would love to be a member."

"Good. After the news, I don't think I'll have any problems finding someone to be your second sponsor. And tell your folks in your public relations unit that next time they put out a press release about the Chicago Police Department helping the FBI, they can mention my name, too. Good publicity is never a bad thing." Now Bill was laughing, too.

All was right in his world. Today. Tomorrow might bring new challenges. But Chicago was now home for Bill and his family, and he was prepared to do whatever necessary to keep the town safe.

Chapter 37

Saturday, September 12th

The Iranian Ambassador to the United Nations had been invited to meet with the United States Ambassador to the UN. This was highly unusual, and to make it even more strange the meeting was set for 2:00 on a Saturday afternoon, when the UN Building was nearly deserted. The Iranian Ambassador Extraordinary and Plenipotentiary, Majid Takht-Ravanchi, walked into the United States' offices right at 2:00. He was surprised to find a gentleman he didn't know sitting at the receptionist's desk. The gentleman stood, showing proper deference. "Please go on in, Mr. Ambassador."

Majid walked into the inner office, expecting to find his counterpart from the United States. Instead, behind the desk sat the President of the United States! Majid's jaw dropped. "Mr. President? What are you doing here?"

"Please sit down, Mr. Ambassador." Majid took a seat across the desk from the President, still dumfounded.

The President looked at Majid for a moment, and then started. "I invited you here to give you a message for you to pass on to Ruhollah Khomeini. You probably don't know this, and I'm sure you'll try and deny it, but we have irrefutable proof that Iran smuggled weapons of mass destruction into the United States, with the intent of blowing up our Republican and Democratic National Conventions." Majid started to sputter, but the President held up his hand to silence him.

"Our policy on WMDs is to respond in kind. So, what we've done is taken the same bomb you sent us, refined it, smuggled it back into Iran, and buried it within striking distance of Khomeini's home. I'm sure you'll have people looking for it, but it won't do you any good. We know what we're doing. Your government now has a choice. You can come to the negotiations table in Geneva and start seriously talking about nuclear disarmament, and you can stop sponsoring groups like Hezbollah, or we will set off that bomb, and you can look for a new Supreme Leader. Not to mention that the bomb would take out half of Tehran, and make it uninhabitable for around a hundred years or so. The bomb you sent us was an RDD, and that same radioactive material is now buried in your capital. Come to the table, or I have no problem setting off the bomb. And if you don't believe me, just watch the news in the next hour or so."

The President stood up, and walked out without shaking hands with the Ambassador. Majid thought to himself, "I've never been treated so rudely by a head of state in my life." But then he reflected on the President's words, and realized that the President was serious, and spitting mad. Majid didn't know about the bombs, but he realized that Khomeini was probably willing to try such a stunt. Majid got up and walked out. There was no one in the outer office.

Chapter 38

Sunday, September 13th

2:00 on a Saturday afternoon in New York meant that it was 3:00 Sunday morning in Pyongyang. The modified B-2 Spirit Stealth Bomber was so stealthy that even United States radar couldn't hardly track it. So, the North Koreans didn't have a chance. The plane had taken off from its base at Hurlburt Field, in the Florida panhandle, and flown non-stop nearly 18,000 miles, going the long way around the world across the Pacific, with two mid-air refuelings along the way.

The President of the United States has issued a Finding, which meant that it was his order that the bomb the North Koreans had planted in Chicago be returned to sender. The target was Ryongsong, loosely translated as "Central Luxury Mansion," the main home of Kim Jong-un. Internet traffic had confirmed the schedule that General Shin had provided, showing that Kim was home.

The bomb the Koreans has supplied had been cut down in size. The United States didn't want to blow up half of Pyongyang, but just get rid of Kim. The residence was located by the plane's computers, and a laser designator placed on the center of the residence. The place was opulent, but not hardened at all against bombs. The bomb bay doors opened on the plane, and that did allow for a short radar hit. But the bomb bay doors were only open for about five seconds, and closed immediately when the bomb was released. One of the radar operators on the ground, on his usual shift at a site south of town, said, "Did you see that blip on the screen?

"Nah," said his partner. "Probably just birds." The North Koreans didn't have recording capability on their defensive radars – too expensive to buy or steal that software – so there was no record of the possible blip.

A minute later the bomb hit, and Ryongsong, along with the Supreme Leader of North Korea, ceased to exist.

It took about an hour for news to start leaking out of North Korea. The South Koreans had listening posts all along the demilitarized zone, and they started picking up chatter about the explosion almost immediately. South Korea quickly went to a higher defense level, expecting the North Koreans to blame the South and retaliate. But there was too much confusion in North Korea, and it took time for order to be restored. By morning, it was obvious that Kim was dead. Too many people in the North Korean military were talking about it over the radio. At noon, Korean Time, there was an announcement.

We are sad to announce that our beloved Supreme Leader, Kim Jong-un, has passed away unexpectedly. We have established a military junta of four generals to temporarily lead the People's Republic, until we can determine how best to proceed. We will announce funeral service information as soon as it is available.

China was asked to help investigate the bomb, since the North Koreans did not have the CSI infrastructure to try and determine the bomb's origins. The Chinese almost immediately discovered that the tracers in the cesium-137 scattered around the remains of the palace showed that the radioactive material came from Hong Kong hospitals. A quick investigation there determined that a Triad had been selling that cesium to North Korea. So, the Chinese backed out, telling the North Koreans that the bomb originated in their own country. A few scientists were interrogated, some until they died, but all the officials learned was that the scientists had worked to mix the radioactive material with other plastic explosives. The only person that knew the entire picture was General Shin, and he was in Los Angeles, applying for a teaching position at UCLA. The North Koreans were at a loss as to how the bomb got to Ryongsong, and who placed it there. But some people suspected.

A few days later the military group in charge of North Korea made another announcement:

It is time for the People's Republic to take our true place in world affairs. The draconian policies of the previous regime have resulted in nothing but starvation and ruin for a large part of our population. So, effective immediately, we are shutting down our entire nuclear program, and we will

welcome United Nations inspectors to our country to prove that is the case. We hope that the rest of the world will see this as a gesture of goodwill, and that other nations will eliminate the horrible sanctions that have hurt our people so badly.

We also want to start looking at the possibility of opening talks with our neighbor to the south. We are really one people, and we need to look at an open border, trade possibilities, and economic partnerships that would benefit us both. There should not be a South Korea and North Korea, but just Korea, and we should all work towards that goal.

Chapter 39

Monday, September 14th

The New York Times

Flash - Iran has announced that they are willing to resume talks in Geneva on nuclear non-proliferation possibilities. They are sending a new team of negotiators to that city, and talks may begin as early as October 1st.

Bill Peterson read the newsflash, and smiled to himself. He thought about his alma mater, The University of Texas, and the University's slogan – "What starts here changes the world." Maybe this time they were right.

ACKNOWLEDGEMENTS

A special thanks to Brad Wade, Chief of Police in Grant, Michigan, for his help on how the Grant part of this story might develop.

And as usual, thanks to Joanna Davis, the best editor in the business.

While there are several "real" people used as characters in this book, all their actions, and the events and timelines used in this book are fictional. Some buildings and places have been moved to fit the story. Any errors in the story are mine.

Thanks for reading, and I hope you enjoyed the book. If you liked this one, there are currently two other Bill Peterson books in publication.

And if you *really* liked this one, please leave me a review on Amazon!

- Jerry Johnson